HIGHLAND FORTITUDE
The Band of Cousins, Book 5
Copyright © 2018 by Keira Montclair

Cover Design and Interior Format
©  KILLION
GROUP, INC.

HIGHLAND FORTITUDE

5 THE BAND OF COUSINS

KEIRA MONTCLAIR

THE GRANTS AND RAMSAYS

FAMILY TREE (1280s)

——◆——

GRANTS

LAIRD ALEXANDER GRANT and wife, MADDIE
John (Jake) and wife, Aline
James (Jamie) and wife, Gracie
Kyla and husband, Finlay
Connor
Elizabeth
Maeve

BRENNA GRANT and husband, QUADE RAMSAY
Torrian (Quade's son from his first marriage) and wife,
Heather—daughter, Nellie (Heather's daughter from a
previous relationship) and son, Lachlan
Lily (Quade's daughter from his first marriage) and hus-
band, Kyle—twin daughters, Lise and Liliana
Bethia and husband, Donnan—son, Drystan
Gregor
Jennet
Geva (adopted)
Emma (adopted)

ROBBIE GRANT and wife, CARALYN
Ashlyn (Caralyn's daughter from a previous relationship)
and husband, Magnus—daughter, X
Gracie (Caralyn's daughter from a previous relationship)
and husband, Jamie

Rodric (Roddy) and wife, Rose
Padraig

BRODIE GRANT and wife, CELESTINA
Loki (adopted) and wife, Arabella—sons, Kenzie (adopted) and Lucas, daughter, Ami (adopted)
Braden and wife, Cairstine—son, Steenie (Cairstine's son from previous relationship)
Catriona
Alison

JENNIE GRANT and husband, AEDAN CAMERON
Riley
Tara
Brin

RAMSAYS

QUADE RAMSAY and wife, BRENNA GRANT
Torrian (Quade's son from his first marriage) and wife,
Heather—Nellie (Heather's daughter from a previous rela-
tionship) and son, Lachlan
Lily (Quade's daughter from his first marriage) and hus-
band, Kyle—twin daughters, Lise and Liliana
Bethia and husband, Donnan
Gregor
Jennet

LOGAN RAMSAY and wife, GWYNETH
Molly (adopted) and husband, Tormod
Maggie (adopted)
Sorcha and husband, Cailean
Gavin
Brigid

MICHEIL RAMSAY and wife, DIANA
David
Daniel

AVELINA RAMSAY and DREW MENZIE
Elyse
Tad
Tomag
Maitland

CHAPTER ONE

———◆———

Autumn 1284, the Highlands of Scotland

HE COULDN'T LET HER GO.

Daniel Drummond tugged on the reins of his horse, branches slapping at his face because the beast balked, but he persisted. "We're going back. I cannot leave her."

Constance was the first lass he'd ever cared about this much…so much it hurt. She'd told him she wished to become a nun. He'd intended to respect her wishes, but now that the time had come to walk away, he just couldn't do it. What if he never saw her again?

They'd met while Daniel and his cousins were in pursuit of the Channel of Dubh, a network of unscrupulous men that sold lasses across the seas. Roddy had fallen in love with Constance's friend, Rose, a novice whose mother was involved in the network, and in helping Roddy, Daniel had spent time with the lass's lovely friend. They'd been through some traumatic events together, but all had ended well—the wicked men and women helping the network had been killed or arrested and the novices they'd preyed upon had been saved. Roddy and Rose had married and returned to Grant land, and Daniel and a few of his cousins had stayed behind to ensure the abbey settled from the turmoil. Daniel had visited daily in the interim, seeking out Constance whenever he did, but the moment he'd dreaded had finally come.

He no longer had any reason to visit the abbey.

All was well in the area, and he needed to return home, but as soon as he began to ride east, the truth had hit him hard.

He'd left too soon. He hadn't said a word about how he felt, and he didn't wish to spend a lifetime regretting his actions.

Even if they had no hope of a future, he had to know if she felt the same way.

He pushed his horse through the rain, slopping down the muddy path as fast as he could. When he arrived, he led his horse to the stables around the back, his chest heaving nearly as much as his horse's. He patted the beast's withers. "Good job, my friend. I promise to find you an apple when I return."

He reached the front gates and barreled through them, the guards saying nothing because he'd just left. Bounding toward the side door of the abbey, he flipped the drenched hair out of his eyes and flung the door open, standing inside the foyer until his eyes adjusted, the water drenching the floor he stood upon. His heart raced for fear he'd be rejected, but at least she would see him. He was certain of that.

Daniel glanced up and down the passageway, but it was empty. He took two deep breaths, hoping to calm the storm racing through his body. Uncertainty had a way of doing this to him.

Did he have a chance?

"Constance? Where are you?" he yelled, not caring what the nuns would say.

A red-haired lass, her long curls falling over her shoulders, appeared out of the door at the end of the corridor. "Daniel? What is it?"

Her beauty nearly took his breath away, much as it always did. The mass of dark red hair, the dash of freckles across the bridge of her nose, the lilt of her voice, and her positive attitude all served to lift his spirits. He needed her in his life—desperately. Her essence always washed over him like the earliest spring breeze, promising warmth, birdsong, and sunshine to follow.

How could he walk away and leave her forever?

Daniel took a deep breath and strode down the passageway. "I'm not going away. I want you, Constance. I like you, mayhap I even love you. I know you intend to stay here, but I couldn't leave without telling you I want you in my life." He stood in front of her, panting, and stared down at her beautiful face. Her face was tipped up to him, her eyes on his. He'd hoped to see some indication his feelings were returned, but her expression was unreadable.

"Constance…" He grabbed her hip, tugging her close, and she squealed and wrapped her hands around his biceps.

"Constance, if you don't wish to be kissed, you better say so now, because once I start, I may never let you go."

Then he knew. Her eyes assessed him with something different, and deeper, than surprise and she parted her lips and said, "Do not stop."

His lips descended on hers with a growl. He ravaged her mouth, his hunger for her overpowering his thoughts. Had he had any sense, he would have approached her more cautiously, with a tender kiss, but he'd dreamed of this moment ever since they met.

"Constance," he rasped. "I should slow down, but you make me daft with need."

Her response was to thread her fingers through his hair and hold on tight, tugging him back for more. She kissed him with abandon, parting her lips to give him access to the deepest crevices of her mouth. His tongue delved deep, teasing her, stroking her until she moaned, and suddenly she gasped for breath. When she tipped her head back, he took advantage of her position to ravage her neck, kissing a trail down to the neck of her gown.

She whimpered as she clung to him, her body plastered against his wet clothing in a sensual tease that made him wish to strip down and tear the clothes from her body. He longed to bury himself deep inside her and never let her go again.

Aye, he was sure of it now. They belonged together, forever.

"Constance!"

Constance stumbled back, and Daniel caught her before she lost her balance completely. "Aye, Sister Murreall." She turned to face the nun, whose face and neck were red with fury. "Forgive me. I lost myself."

Daniel kept his hand at the small of her back in case she lost her balance again. "Sister, 'twas all my fault. I came inside and did not give her a chance to refuse my advances, but I love her."

"Young man, I understand you were a part of the group of warriors that saved our lasses from being sold across the seas. We granted you the freedom to come and go from the abbey for several days, but that does not give you license to attack our novices. Constance, I came to get you because Mother Abbess wishes to see you in her office. Please do not dally."

Constance dropped her gaze to stare at the floor, clearly ashamed of her actions.

When Daniel didn't leave at once, the nun turned toward him with a swish of her hand and said, "Begone, lad."

Daniel forced himself to leave, though he mouthed the words, "I'll be back," at Constance as soon as the nun had her back turned. She glanced at him, her eyes sparkling, before she followed the nun as she'd been instructed. That wee green sparkle gave him hope.

He stepped back outside, discouraged to see the heavy rain continued, but the weather wouldn't keep him away. Once the sun dropped, he'd find her again inside the abbey—no guard could keep him out.

———➤———

CONSTANCE FOLLOWED THE NUN DOWN the passageway, the sister's silence grating on her nerves more than if a squawking bird had been perched on her shoulder pecking at her ear. Her thoughts were muddled, and no wonder—she didn't know if she'd ever be normal again after that onslaught of maleness and passion.

Daniel had returned to the abbey for her.

For her!

What a sight he'd looked, his clothes plastered to his muscular chest from the rain, his eyes full of passion. She'd been kissed before, but never like that. Why, it was a wonder she hadn't melted in a puddle at Daniel's feet. She reached into the pocket sewn into her novice's gown and rubbed the dark red stone she kept hidden there. Her good luck charm had served her well. She'd hoped he would return at least one more time, and so he had.

Her feelings for Daniel were stronger than anything she'd ever experienced before. She wasn't ready to have him walk away forever.

Once they reached Mother Abbess's chamber, Sister Murreall told her to stay in the corridor and entered the room alone. Constance's cheeks burned as she listened to the murmuring voices, knowing the nun was telling the abbess about Daniel. Would her trials and tribulations never end? Finally, Sister Murreall reappeared and nodded for her to enter the chamber. Despite her shame, she kept her head high as she sat in the chair across from the woman's desk.

"Forgive me, Mother Abbess. I was caught up in the moment. 'Twas my fault and 'twill never happen again." She folded her hands in her lap and allowed her gaze to settle on her now twiddling fingers, doing her best to look contrite. Would she be forgiven this one time or punished and sent to the cellars?

Mother Abbess sighed. "Child, I understand you've been through some trying times. Those lads from Clan Ramsay and Clan Grant did an admirable deed when they saved Rose and our other lasses from being sold across the water. Even so, they are lads like any others and do not belong on a pedestal. You are here to take your vows as a nun, to become a novice, or have you forgotten your purpose in life?"

Constance lifted her gaze and stared at the wall next to her. What should she do? True, she desperately needed to hide, but was she prepared to take her vows? At one time she'd considered the nunnery the only safe place for her, but now she wasn't so sure. After all, if Daniel and his friends hadn't intervened, she and the other lasses might have suffered a horrible fate. What if she changed her mind? "Forgive me, Mother Abbess, I am confused at the moment."

The older woman clucked her tongue. "As anyone would be in your position, my dear. I'm sure it also weighs on you that you've lost your dear friend. Rose has found her voice and married Roddy Grant. I could not be more pleased for her happiness. Do you also wish to marry? Have you changed your mind?"

She shook her head, doing her best to choke her tears down. "I'm not sure."

"You need not make a decision right away. You have plenty of time before you will be asked to take your vows. You are one of the few who can read, so I ask that you study the Bible and beg for forgiveness for your transgressions. This will help you to learn God's way—and His will."

Constance was so confused and flustered she couldn't even look at the abbess. She didn't know what she wanted.

The abbess continued, "While you search your soul, will you not consider being truthful with me?"

Constance jerked her gaze back to the abbess's. "Truthful? I don't understand." Her hands began to tremble, so she clasped them together in an attempt to hide the fine movement.

"Lass, you've told us that your family could no longer feed you because you had seven brothers and sisters. Yet you've had no contact from anyone in your family. Indeed, you've had no missives or visitors at all. My suspicions tell me there is much more to your story than you've told us."

"I don't know what you mean, Mother Abbess," she stuttered. "May I please be excused? I suddenly feel ill, like I may be sick. I…" She bolted out of her seat, freezing in her spot as she awaited permission to leave.

"Aye, you may take your leave, lass. I pray you will think on what I've said." Her kind eyes gave Constance solace. When she'd first met the small, rotund woman, she'd been afraid of her, but Mother Marion had a warm heart. Still, she could be quite strict when necessary. She prayed the abbess wouldn't continue to press her about her background.

Because Constance wouldn't be able to tell the truth. Her very life might depend on her ability to lie.

She turned and raced out the door and down the passageway toward her chamber. She wished Rose or Daniel were here to console her.

More than anything, she wished for her dear mother.

She wanted to go home.

However, that was quite impossible.

CHAPTER TWO

———◆———

DANIEL PACED IN A CLEARING less than an hour from the abbey. He had to see Constance again. He had to find out if she still planned on taking her vows. If she wasn't certain she wanted to be a nun, mayhap she'd agree to go to Braden's castle with him. The best thing he could do right now was get her away from the abbey to see if they would suit. The abbey was no environment for romance. The red-faced nun was proof of that.

Maybe she'd give him a chance to court her.

God's bones, but he loved her. Tasting her, feeling her in his arms—it had convinced him they had a special connection, something most other people never found.

He shouldn't have kissed her the way he had. He'd held her so tight it was a wonder she hadn't pushed him away.

But she hadn't. She'd deepened their kiss and pulled him closer. They had a passion together that was uncontestable, just as strong as he'd guessed.

As he'd hoped.

He and his cousins had just saved seven lasses bound for Western Europe on a galley ship. Their group, which they'd named the Band of Cousins, aimed to put an end to the sale of young lasses and lads to unscrupulous bidders across the water. Their latest success was due to the efforts of his cousin, Roddy, who'd fallen in love with Constance's friend, Rose MacDole. They'd discovered Rose's mother, Lady MacDole, and a priest from the abbey were involved in a wicked scheme to sell young novices through the Channel of Dubh, a network that harbored and sold unknowing lasses for coin. The abbess had been devastated to learn some of the lasses under her care had been so mistreated.

Rose had married Roddy at the abbey and departed less than a sennight ago for Roddy's homeland, Clan Grant. Daniel and his other cousins had stayed to ensure the network at the abbey was properly put to rest. Will and Maggie had escorted the villains to the magistrate. Connor, Gavin, and Gregor had gone on to Braden's keep, Muir Castle, to celebrate. They'd judged this day to be the end of their most recent venture with the Band of Cousins. He'd join them on the morrow.

How he wished he could convince Constance to come with him.

He knew what they'd say if he told them of his interest in the lass.

They'd say he was too young. Aye, he was only seven and ten, but this winter he'd be eight and ten, plenty old enough to marry. If he found his partner in life, why wait? They could grow old together.

He recalled his sire saying he'd fallen in love with his mother nearly the first day they had met. She'd taken him on a daft dash after some English knight she'd thought she fancied in Edinburgh, but in the end, she'd fallen in love with Daniel's sire and married him.

His father's persistence had paid off. He recalled the number of times that his sire had taunted his mother, claiming if he hadn't stayed by her side that she would have relinquished her father's castle and land in favor of some hovel in England. Instead, she was one of the few female clan chieftains in Scotland.

She was a fine leader. His clan prospered unlike many others.

Micheil Ramsay had been wise to stand by the woman

he loved. Daniel Drummond would not leave Constance either. Something was bothering the lass and he vowed to help her and stand by her side.

No matter what it took. When he crept back into the abbey in the darkest of the night, they would talk. That's what they needed to do.

He had to convince her to follow him.

———————

CONSTANCE FOUND HER WAY DOWN the stairs and out the back door to the gardens. It was nearly midnight, and no one was about. The entire abbey had been in such a turmoil since the return of the kidnapped lasses—everyone had retired early. There had been few sessions of silent prayer, but mostly because the novices were incapable of sitting quietly.

Constance knew just how they felt. She was more unsettled than ever. The abbess knew she had a secret, and Daniel's kiss had made her doubt everything.

Daniel made her feel like no other lad had. He made her feel alive and special, something that being one of eight children certainly hadn't done.

She couldn't forget that he'd promised to return. And he would. Daniel's friend called him "Ghost" for a reason—he could sneak past any gate, any closed door. A smile crossed her face as she thought about how much he enjoyed the challenge, the threat of discovery, and the success of victory. Because she was desperate to see him, too much so to leave it to chance, she'd decided to make it easy on him and wait at the bench at the back of the property, the same place where Roddy and Rose had fallen in love.

If it had worked magic for them, perhaps it could also work for her.

Less than an hour later, something dropped in front of her, startling her enough to jump out of her seat and search the area for an intruder, but she saw no one. A few moments later, something flew through the air and landed at her feet. Curious, she bent over and picked it up.

A hazelnut. They kept landing at her feet until she had six in her hand. She couldn't stop the wide grin on her face because she was quite sure she knew who had thrown them. "Show yourself or I'll go in, because if you are not Daniel, I don't wish to see you." She waited a few moments until a rustling sound stirred the hedge behind her, then Daniel's face popped in between the branches.

"You called for me, lass?" He winked, a devilish grin on his face.

"Aye, Daniel," she whispered. "Get over here before you're seen, and I get into more trouble."

He leaped over the hedge and landed a few steps away from her. She expected another passionate kiss, but to her surprise he gave her a quick peck on the lips before he stepped back. "No more ravishing of innocent lassies, I promise, Constance."

She wiggled her nose and whispered, "Why not? I liked it." She giggled and he whipped his hand out from behind his back, thrusting a cluster of weeds, twigs with berries, and a few flowers into her hands. "Only the verra best for you, my sweet bluebell."

Extending her hand to accept the gift, she brought the bouquet up to her nose and inhaled deeply, then she said, "These are the most beautiful flowers I've ever received, Daniel. My thanks to you." She fluttered her eyelashes at him, but he didn't catch on.

"How many bouquets of weeds and sticks have you received?"

"That is not important," she said, clutching the flowers to her chest. "They are lovely. I shall keep them forever."

He reached for the bouquet, but she tugged it close.

He reached again and explained, "I just wish to show you there was one bluebell inside. It made me think of you, sweet one." He fiddled with the stalks and pulled out one flower that had fallen over limp already. "See? A bluebell, even if 'tis nearly dead."

She laughed, a husky trill to her voice. "Daniel, bluebells don't grow this time of year. It looks more like a coneflower."

"'Tis blue and a flower, is it not? Close enough to a bluebell. I admit I'm not an expert on flowers."

She couldn't ruin his good deed. "I must be wrong. Perhaps 'tis indeed a bluebell." She leaned toward him and gave him a chaste kiss on his cheek, lingering just a bit to take in his manly scent.

He set her away from him. "Enough or you'll get me in trouble." His gaze narrowed as it caught hers. "I came to chat. Come sit on the bench with me."

She sighed but nodded and allowed him to usher her over to the bench. Once she was settled, he sat down next to her. "What must we talk about?" she asked, pushing her lower lip out in a pout, still clutching her bouquet. "I prefer kisses."

He kissed her temple and said, "There, one kiss. Will you come to Braden Grant's castle with me for a brief visit?"

"Daniel," she said, rubbing her forehead in frustration. "I doubt it would be allowed. They are quite strict here about visitations, probably more so after the disaster we just had." She stared at the flowers in her lap, fiddling with them so she wouldn't have to look at him. In truth, she couldn't risk being seen outside the abbey. If she ran into the wrong person…Well, she wouldn't give that thought much consideration because she couldn't let it happen.

She could *not* get caught.

"I promise I'll have you back within a sennight." He tucked a stray hair behind her ear. "You could ask permission, could you not? We'll just say we're celebrating the end of the tyranny that was Jean MacDole."

"Will Rose be there?"

He shook his head. "Nay, she's gone on to Clan Grant

to meet Roddy's family. But there are many members of Clan Grant at Roddy's house presently. I'll be staying on there for a wee bit, if they'll still have me. You would like Braden's wife, Cairstine."

The picture he painted was a bonny one. Could she dare risk it?

Then he smiled at her, his eyes twinkling, and she knew her answer.

"I will ask, but only under one condition." She wiggled her bottom on the bench. Daniel made her do things she just didn't understand.

"Good. Name it and I'll do it if I can."

"Your hand. Tell me what happened to your hand. You promised." The first time they'd met, Daniel had been helping Roddy and Rose. She'd taken one look at his arm, noticed his missing hand, and blurted out, "What happened to your hand?" Daniel had pretended to be shocked, saying he didn't know where he'd lost it or some other silly response, but that was Daniel. He'd promised to tell her the truth later.

"I promised I'd tell you if you came to Clan Grant. That was the wager." He paused to think for a moment, then said, "But I'll consider Braden as close enough to Clan Grants. If you visit his castle, I'll tell you." He crossed his arms, not willing to share his hidden secret yet.

She glanced at the long sleeve covering his stump. He'd lost his left hand just above the wrist. "Nay, if you wish for me to come with you, you must tell me now." Her imagination had run wild. Part of her worried he might have been injured as a punishment for stealing or committing some other sort of crime. She couldn't shake the notion that finding out how he'd lost his hand would tell her something important about him.

He stared up at the night sky and brushed his hair out of his face. "All right. I'll tell you, but give me a moment."

She guessed this had to be difficult for him. Daniel was a

very handsome man. His hair was a deep and rich mahogany, touched by just a hint of red, and his unblemished skin was tan from the sun, a testament to how much time he spent outside. His forest green eyes, surrounded by thick lashes, sparkled with humor. In fact, Daniel's appearance was very nearly perfect, until one's gaze traveled lower, past his powerful biceps and broad chest to his left side. The shock of not seeing another hand there had caught her off guard the first time, making her stare at the scarred stump below his elbow. The scars weren't visible this eve because of the tunic he wore. She couldn't help but wonder how painful it had been. How he'd learned to adjust to such a shocking loss.

"Tell me, Daniel. Please?" She reached for his scarred arm, pushing the sleeve of his tunic up. "I need to know this about you."

CHAPTER THREE

D ANIEL CLOSED HIS EYES FOR just a second, taking his mind off the beautiful lass in front of him, and mentally returned to the day it had happened.

It. That's what he always called the disfiguring incident. *It.*

It had happened on a hot day in the summer. They'd had so few warm days that summer, and he and his friend had decided to defy his parents and go to the loch for a swim. They'd been forbidden to leave the castle grounds because reivers were roaming the area. Two of their clanmates had been slain, and his sire had sent out a force of warriors to find them. No person under the age of ten and five was supposed to leave the castle walls until the culprits were caught and punished.

Daniel and his friend had waited until the guards were out of sight before they snuck outside the curtain wall.

A quick dip was all they'd wanted. Something to cool themselves down in the heat.

He hadn't even told his brother where he was going…

Constance took ahold of the stub of his arm and caressed his scars. He stared at her in shock. When had anyone other than his parents ever touched his wound?

"I was six winters when my friend and I snuck out to the loch. My sire had taken a patrol of guards out to search for a band of reivers who were causing trouble on our land. My parents had forbidden us to go outside the curtain wall until the reivers were found."

"You found them," Constance stated.

"Actually, they found us. I was just about to dive in after my friend when we heard the horses. I tried to get back to my horse before they reached us, but my friend was oblivious to the danger, and I wasted time trying to alert him. When they finally reached us, one of the reivers grabbed my friend by the shoulders and held him underwater. I managed to get to my sword. Instead of running, I foolishly tried to protect myself when the reiver came at me. He played with me for a while, taunting me about my small sword and asking me to swing it. I just kept backing up."

He paused, savoring Constance's touch, and then said, "Things might have ended differently had my brother not followed us out. David had to go save my friend first because the bastard was drowning him. Once he came to my assistance, the reiver stopped taunting me and swung his sword down, cutting my hand off in an instant. David hadn't reached my side yet, so there was naught he could do."

"Oh, Daniel," Constance said, swiping at the tears that erupted on her face. "How terrible."

"I don't remember much after that. My brother saved my life, or so my aunts told me, because he tied his plaid above my elbow, which stemmed the bleeding. The oddest thing was that my fingers hurt even though they weren't there anymore. At first, I was furious. Mad at everyone around me, but then I noticed my brother. He considered it his failure. He's three years older than me, and I heard him crying one day, telling my mother 'twas his fault because he'd gone to save my friend instead of me. I hadn't considered how the entire incident would affect other people, but the more I looked around, the more I saw the pain in their eyes.

"So I decided to stop feeling sorry for myself and started

training in the lists with my brother. I vowed to make up for my loss by building my muscles and learning to swing my sword with only one hand."

"I'm so sorry, Daniel," Constance said, reaching for his hand and squeezing it. He recognized the look in her eyes—pity. He didn't want her pity, and he almost drew away on instinct, but she kept speaking. "You were too young to blame yourself. 'Tis how I feel. Is David your only sibling?"

"Aye. He'll take over the lairdship after my mother, Diana Drummond."

"You're one of those Drummonds? The ones whose laird is a woman?"

"Aye, the one whose mother is laird. I have wonderful parents. Tell me more about your family. Where are you from?"

"A long way from here. My parents have eight bairns. They couldn't feed us all so they gave two of us away. I came to Sona Abbey. My brother wishes to be a monk and went to a different abbey."

"Seven brothers and sisters. How fortunate you are. I'd like to hear more about them, but first, I held up my part of the bargain, now 'tis your turn. Talk to the abbess on the morrow. Shall I come for you when the sun is highest?"

"I'll talk with her. All of us were upset by what happened with the other lasses. They've suggested it might serve us well to take a journey home for a time to overcome the ordeal. Mayhap they'll allow me to travel with you instead, but you'll need to bring guards with you, or she'll never allow me to go."

He jumped up, leaned over to plant a kiss on her lips, then said, "Perfect. I'll escort you to your corridor, my dear, then I shall return on the morrow, midday."

"No more kisses?"

"Nay. I'll not risk getting barred from your presence." He hurried her over to the building, and before he opened the door, he whispered close to her ear, "But we'll have plenty of time at Braden's to get to know each other better. I promise."

If pity was what it took for her to give him a chance, he'd accept it for now.

———◆———

CONSTANCE RODE IN FRONT OF Daniel to Muir Castle, where Braden Grant and his wife, Cairstine, lived. She was surprised the abbess had allowed her this visit. While the older women had been hesitant, especially after the incident with Daniel, Brodie Grant, brother to the famous Alexander Grant, had accompanied Daniel to the abbey and met with the abbess. Somehow he'd managed to convince her to send Constance with them, promising she would be returned within a sennight.

She leaned back against Daniel, taking in his scent of pine and horse with a touch of mint from the leaves he'd been chewing. They hadn't said much to each other— she'd instead used the opportunity to get as close to him as possible, sighing with each small comfort he offered her— the touch of his hand on her hip, the whisper of his breath against her ear, and the clench of his thighs aimed to keep her in place as they cantered on horseback through the Highlands. It had been an unusually warm autumn, and the trees still boasted many colorful leaves, much to her delight. She hated when they all fell off at the beginning of winter. The cool breeze whistled through the trees, sending another handful of leaves to the ground, rustling as they landed.

The scenery was forever changing in the Highlands, and she loved it. As soon as she admired the changing of the leaves, they'd move down the path only to be surrounded by a forest of pines, the green of the needles and the scent overwhelming her senses.

What better place could there be than inside Daniel's

arms enjoying the beauty of the Highlands? Though she was taking a risk by riding out in the open, away from the abbey, there was no doubt in her mind she would be safe at Muir Castle with all the Grants at the keep. She closed her eyes and relaxed against him, pleased to be away from the abbey, if only for a short time.

Once they arrived, Daniel assisted her down from the horse, but she stumbled and fell against him. He caught her with his right arm. "I think you fell asleep, lass."

Constance muttered, "Did I?" She didn't wish to admit how comfortable she'd been pressed against him, but she also didn't lie easily so she felt an evasion was the best way to answer.

Up until she'd come to the abbey, she'd never told a lie. Why did they come so easily of late?

The answer was simple. Protection. She had to protect herself since no one else would.

Introductions were made quickly around the hall. A woman named Aunt Fina announced, "We've goblets of ale for all. Platters of cheese and loaves of bread will follow. Make yourselves at home."

Cairstine, Braden's wife, approached her with a smile. "Why don't I show you to your chamber, Constance? I'm sure you'd like a rest before you eat."

She glanced at Daniel, who waved her on. "Freshen up, if you like. Do as you wish here. No one will give you orders or chores to do, I promise."

Constance caught him looking at her as she followed Cairstine up the stairs. "'Tis a lovely chamber," Cairstine said, leading her down the passageway to a chamber at the end, "but it has not been used in a while."

"I feel better that I'm not taking anyone's chamber. I…" Constance almost gave herself away, ready to confess something she knew about the nobility, but she caught herself in time. She couldn't let anyone know about her background.

"Hilda just cleaned it," Cairstine said as she opened the door and stood back. "She's insisted on cleaning everything. It has fresh linens as well. I'll send fresh water up for you."

A set of footsteps echoed down the corridor as if the person were running.

Cairstine smiled. "That must be my son, Steenie. He gets quite excited when we have company."

Steenie, a wee lad with bright eyes, came flying into the chamber. "Mama! We have guests."

He froze as soon as his gaze landed on Constance. "You found her."

Cairstine clucked her tongue. "Steenie, where are your manners?"

He stopped, folded his hands in front of him and said, "Greetings, my lady, and welcome to Muir Castle." He paused for a moment before he continued on in a typical childlike ramble of saying everything that popped into his mind. "We never had to do this when my real da was here, Mama. Why now?"

"You know why, laddie. Please do not be rude to our guest."

He dropped his gaze to the floor. "My apologies, Mama. I like it better now, too. 'Tis a most happy place, unlike before." He rushed over and squeezed his mother. "I love you, Mama. Greetings to your friend. May I go see Paddy and Corc again? He needs help with the new horses."

Cairstine said, "Off with you. Pay attention to Corc."

By then, Steenie was already barreling down the staircase, but he replied with a shout, "I will, Mama."

Constance couldn't help but giggle. "He's a sweet laddie."

"Poor Steenie has had quite an adjustment to make, though 'tis all for the best. 'Tis a long story, but we were blessed the day Braden Grant walked into our lives. My clan was Clan Muir."

Constance nodded, deciding to set her questions aside.

Cairstine was a lovely woman, and their castle was very nice. "Braden was involved with the issue at the sea loch?"

"Aye, he was. What a terrible situation. You were not on the boat, were you? Poor Rose. What a fright it must have been." Cairstine kneaded her hands and fussed with the furs on the bed.

"I was not on the boat, but I was there. I'd never been so frightened in all my life."

Cairstine patted her hands. "You need not be frightened any longer. I hope you enjoy your stay here. We are small, but Steenie keeps everything lively, and we have two wonderful cooks. Mayhap you can help me prepare the garden for next spring, if you'd like." She headed over to the door. "I'll send an urn of water up for you. Take your time, and if there is anything you need, I'd be glad to help." Then she left, closing the door behind her.

Constance flopped onto the bed, worried now. She'd been so excited to leave the abbey, but it struck her that she'd need to lie about her past. Convincingly. To a lot of people.

She would not go back downstairs until she had a story completely formed in her mind. She'd have to create a new life, then go over it and over it lest she forget it.

That was the only way she'd get away with her lie.

CHAPTER FOUR

———

D ANIEL WANDERED OUTSIDE TOWARD THE stables early the next morn. Constance hadn't come back down to the great hall last eve. Cairstine had said she'd seemed exhausted, and his cousins Braden and Connor had agreed—and after all she'd been through, she deserved the chance to sleep as long as she needed.

Daniel couldn't argue with that, but he'd hated to lose even one night. He wished to get to know her better. "Corc," he said to the stablemaster, "I think I'm in need of a horse, just a quick ride to clear my head this morn. I'll get him saddled."

"No worry, lad. I'll saddle the beast for you. He's a fine piece of horse flesh. Are you riding alone, Ghost?" Corc asked, lifting the saddle onto the back of the horse.

Daniel grinned at the man's use of his moniker. The name his cousins had given him never failed to amuse him. He really did have the ability to get in and out of places without being seen, so maybe he deserved it.

He was about to reply to Corc but didn't because he heard the happy lilt of a young lass's voice coming from the keep, followed by a small laugh. Constance. Loud enough for anyone nearby to hear, he cleared his throat and said, "Mayhap not. I'd love the company of a flame-haired beauty. I can hope she's looking for me, can I not, Corc?"

Corc snorted. "If you know the lass's mind, you're smarter

than the rest of us."

Daniel stepped outside and nearly ran into Constance. "Good morn to you, lassie. Where are you off to in such a hurry?"

Steenie came directly behind her. "I brought her out here to meet Paddy the Pony. Follow me, Constance."

Constance shrugged her shoulders and grinned at Daniel, reaching for his hand as they moved through the stables.

Daniel glanced back over his shoulder at the now-smiling Corc, then followed Steenie. "May I meet your pony, also?"

"Aye," Steenie yelled. "He's my best friend. What's your name again?" The lad stopped to peer up at Daniel.

"My name is Daniel."

"What happened to your other hand?" Steenie stared at his missing left hand.

"Steenie," Corc said, following them to the stall. "Be polite." The sparkle in his eyes did not match his admonishing tone.

"May I not ask him?"

Corc cleared his throat, glancing at Daniel for guidance in the matter.

Daniel let go of Constance's hand and crouched down so they were on the same level. "Aye, you may ask me. I lost it in a swordfight when I was six years old. So promise me you'll be careful when you play with real swords?"

Steenie's eyes widened at his revelation. "But I'm only five. You were in a swordfight when you were six?"

"I shouldn't have been. I went somewhere I wasn't supposed to and a bad man swung his sword at me."

Corc said, "See why you must listen to us and not wander outside the gates when we tell you, laddie?"

"Were you outside the gates?" Steenie asked, still unable to take his eyes from the stump that was Daniel's left appendage.

"Aye, I was indeed," he said, standing back up. "My Papa

forbid me to go, but I did anyway."

Corc let out a low whistle. "Sorry, lad." He clasped Daniel's shoulder. "'Tis a tough way to learn your lesson."

Constance tousled Steenie's hair. "It won't happen to you if you listen to Corc and your parents. You must stay where you are safe. There are some bad people outside castles that hide."

Daniel changed the subject quickly after seeing the look in Steenie's eyes. No need to frighten the poor lad. "Where is that special pony I've heard so much about?"

Steenie hurried down to the last stall and proudly pointed to his pony. "See him? Isn't he beautiful?" He petted Paddy's nose as soon as the wee beast came over to the gate. Then Paddy looked at Daniel and shoved his muzzle at him. When Daniel didn't respond, he pushed him again.

Daniel glanced at Steenie for guidance. "Does he do this often, lad?" Paddy pushed him again.

Steenie giggled. "He wants something to eat."

Daniel searched the stable and found a small bucket of apples nearby. He'd not yet seen a horse that didn't love apples. He strode back to the pony and offered him the treat, and he took it with a whinny.

"'Tis what he wanted, Steenie. You know him well."

Paddy nudged him again, but this time the pony was pushing him toward Constance. Daniel allowed the pony his game, pleased to be closer to Constance in any case, and moved slowly toward her.

Steenie giggled. "He says you like Constance. Paddy can tell you belong together."

Corc waved a hand dismissively. "Pay the beast no mind. He is a bit unusual."

Then Paddy edged over to where Constance stood, nudging her hand that had a grip on the gate. She opened her palm and the small Highland pony nuzzled it.

"He likes you, Constance. See? I told you he would. He's magical." Steenie was quite proud of his pet, and Constance's face had lit up with a look of sheer delight that made Daniel wish to kiss her.

Corc chuckled and mussed the lad's hair. "Lad, we have work to do. Saddle up that mare for Constance while I saddle up Daniel's horse. They wish to go riding."

Constance's eyes widened and she whispered to Daniel, "We do?"

Daniel returned the whisper. "I would love to if you'd join me."

Her smile lit up the stables.

"Can I go with them, Corc?" the wee lad asked, jumping up and down.

"Nay, you have your chores to do, and sometimes lads and lassies like to be alone. Another time, mayhap."

Steenie took Constance's hand and led her over to the stall of a pretty chestnut-colored mare. He glanced at Constance and said, "This mare is the best one. She's my mama's."

"Then she must be quite special." She leaned down to the lad to make her request. "Do you mind if I borrow her?"

"Nay, she does not ride much. She'll be happy to gallop for a change." The lad took off in a different direction before returning with his mama's saddle. His mood had not been the least bit affected by Corc's request that he stay home.

Once Daniel and Constance were both mounted, they rode into the beautiful meadow beyond the gate. He glanced at Constance, pleased to see the smile on her face. He had feared she'd be uncomfortable outside the closed quarters of the abbey, but she looked happy to be free and in his company. What a beautiful sight she made—long locks dancing in the wind, hips bouncing and swaying with the movements of her horse. She was a graceful rider.

Constance tugged on the reins and sent her horse galloping across the meadow, pulling the mare in front of

Daniel with a gleeful laugh. They raced until they reached the other side of the meadow and Daniel pulled his horse up next to Constance's, shouting, "I concede, I concede. You are a fine horsewoman, my lady."

The color drained from Constance's face in an instant, making Daniel wonder what he'd said wrong. "What is it?"

"Naught. I just…why did you say 'my lady'?"

"'Tis a respectful term, my lady."

"But I'm not of noble blood."

He softened his tone. "Mayhap not, but you are quite regal to me."

"Please do not call me something I'm not."

Daniel decided to tuck this odd conversation into the back of his mind to analyze later. For now, he'd agree with her. "All right. Would you like to explore the path down into the valley? 'Tis quite beautiful, especially now that the leaves have changed color."

"I would love that."

"If we find any fruit trees, we'll bring some back for our hosts."

"Agreed," she said.

They continued on a path where they could ride abreast, albeit at a much slower pace, which pleased Daniel. "Tell me about your clan."

———◆———

CONSTANCE TOOK A DEEP BREATH and swallowed. "There's not much to tell. We are not part of a clan. We have our own home in the forest. There are three cottages because my sire's two brothers live next to us to help fight off reivers. We do not have much, but my sire's sister married well, and they live in a wonderful castle. We are not far from them, but my sire prefers to keep away from her clan."

"Names? What clan is your aunt's?"

Constance cut him off quickly before he went any further. She didn't want to give him any information he could double check. "I have three sisters: Sybil, Joan, and Denise. Four brothers: Neville, Gareth, Gilbert, and Noah. Noah and I are the youngest, so we were the two they sent away. The others are helpers to my parents. Sybil, Neville, Gareth, and Joan are already married."

"Do they live near you?"

She stuttered—this was a question she hadn't considered—and then answered, "Aye. They all built huts near us."

"'Tis more than three cottages," he commented, but if he thought her response odd, it didn't show on his face.

"Aye," she mumbled. "I meant there were originally three." Hell, but she was already starting to get caught in her lies. Rather than allow him any more questions, she continued to ramble. "I miss my sisters, dearly." Finally, something that was not a lie.

"Which sister are you closest with? I've always thought it might be nice to have a large family, though I have many cousins to love."

"Denise. We shared everything." She couldn't help but become pensive at the thought of her dear sister. She adored her so.

"Do you all have red hair?"

She laughed. "Nay. Denise and I are so much alike, but her hair is golden with just a bit of red. Sybil's hair is light brown, and Joan's is so fair 'tis nearly white. Denise and I are the only two lasses with freckles."

"Why are they all English names? I thought you were Scottish."

"We are, but my mother was English."

A large bird called out to them, causing Daniel to slow. "I know that sound."

Constance glanced around, suddenly afraid of what was about to happen. That call hadn't come from a bird at all. "I see someone." She went into panic mode and turned her horse around, almost knocking into Daniel in her haste. The fear of recognition was powerful, even though she was far into the Highlands that it was nearly impossible anyone would know her. Her sweet mare snorted, picking up on her change in temperament. "I'm going back," she announced, her voice high and thready.

Daniel followed her, and as he did so, he answered the bird call with one of his own. Sure enough, Constance heard the same sound again, speeding her heart up so much she thought it might explode out of her chest.

Daniel came up next to her. "You've no need to worry, Constance."

Only she *was* worried. She pushed her horse to continue on the path until they were nearly at the meadow. There, she finally slowed her horse. "I'm going to cross the meadow as fast as I can."

Daniel caught up with her and grabbed the reins of her horse. "Nay, slow down. 'Tis only my brother, David. I can see them coming up the path through the trees. I think his wife Anna is with him, also. Please, I must wait for him."

Constance let out the breath she didn't realize she was holding. "All right. I'll wait." Surely Daniel had noticed her peculiar reaction, but he didn't seem intent on pressing her. With any luck, his brother's arrival would distract him.

She waited alongside Daniel, watching his face light up as his brother rode ever closer. How wonderful that the two brothers were so close. It reminded her of Denise, which reminded her again of the situation at home… But as David Drummond rode closer, she banished those thoughts and anchored herself in the present moment. She was to meet Daniel's brother, and she was glad for it.

As the riders came closer, she was struck by the resemblance between Daniel and David. The green eyes that smiled at her were nearly the same as the ones she loved peering into—only they didn't sparkle with quite as much humor. Daniel's brother was taller than him, but not by much, and his hair was a rich shade of brown. Anna's eyes were also green, but her hair was a lovely shade of auburn, as if brown were dancing with red.

"Greetings, David," Daniel shouted as soon as they were within hearing distance. "What brings you so far into the Highlands?" Then he turned serious. "Mama and Papa are hale?"

"Aye, they are both fine. I promised Anna we would take a small journey to visit some of my cousins. We thought Braden's new home would be perfect. Are any of our other cousins still here? We heard you had another successful mission."

"Aye. Greetings to you, Anna." David's wife brought her horse up next to her husband's. "This is Constance. Someone I met at the abbey. She is considering taking her vows—" he shot her a glance, "—although I hope to convince her otherwise. We'll explain later."

They began riding in the direction of Muir Castle, followed by five guards who traveled with David and his wife, as Daniel answered his brother's other questions. "Connor is still here, but Roddy and Rose went back to Grant land. Uncle Brodie and Aunt Celestina will be thrilled to see you." Even though the Grant siblings were technically their cousins through the Drummond side, both boys referred to the older generation as aunts and uncles.

The two brothers chatted on the way back about the latest mission of the Band of Cousins and the mission that had brought Daniel and Constance together. Constance breathed a sigh of relief. Though it was difficult to think about everything they'd gone through, it was preferable to facing questions about her background.

They'd almost made it back to the castle when David asked her a question she hadn't anticipated.

"Constance, what's your sire's name?"

Drat. It was such a simple question, but she hadn't thought that through. She'd come up with a story about her father but hadn't thought to give him a fictional name. She couldn't risk using her real name or her sire's. Daniel was crafty, and she didn't doubt he'd be able to find them. She chewed her bottom lip as she frantically searched for a name that would fool them. It had to be someone they didn't know.

Attempting first to distract them again, she said, "'Tis a most lovely day. Do you not agree?" She would be forced to lie, but she wished she'd taken the time to think more carefully about this. It had to be just the right name so as not to arouse suspicion.

"A fabulous autumn day," Anna agreed. "The views have been spectacular. I love the autumn hues of green, gold, and red."

"Constance?" Daniel persisted. "What is your sire's name?"

Hell, a hundred names bounced about in her head. Without taking the time to think it through, she blurted out one of them, although as soon as the words left her mouth, she realized she'd made a mistake. While her sire made a point of not including the lasses in discussions of battles and clans, she thought she'd heard rumblings about this particular clan.

But it was too late to retract. She'd already said the name loud enough for all to hear.

"Buchan. My sire's name is Glenn Buchan."

CHAPTER FIVE

D ANIEL DID HIS BEST TO hide his surprise at Constance's answer. He and most of his cousins had been
involved in the battle that had caused Glenn of Buchan's
death. She was not Glenn's daughter—of that much he
was certain. What he didn't know was why she had felt the
need to lie.

He'd already sensed there was something she was hiding. Constance was not a natural liar, and it showed. How
much of what she'd said was true? Did she have seven
brothers and sisters? He wished to ask, but he needed to
tread carefully. Something had frightened her, he knew,
and it was likely the reason she'd refused to accompany
Rose to Clan Grant.

He shot a glance at his brother, motioning for him to let
it go, since David would also know she'd shared a falsehood. David agreed and changed the subject. "I'm here to
help the cousins if I can, even if 'tis a small way." Though
he was part of the Band of Cousins, he hadn't traveled with
them for a while.

"We were so happy to hear Braden's news, but we hav-
en't met his wife yet. I'm anxious to visit with Cairstine,"
Anna said. "It sounds as though we've shared similar misfortunes."

Once they made it back to Muir Castle, warm greetings
were shared with the newcomers, and everyone settled in
around the large hearth in the great hall, chatting about

the last mission. David was anxious to hear all the details, and Connor and Braden filled him in with a vigor they all seemed to possess about the Band of Cousins.

But Daniel was distracted, unable to focus on anything beyond Constance. He'd thought he was losing his heart to the lass, but could he trust someone who would lie about something so simple as her sire's name? He wanted David and his wife to like Constance, but he knew his brother would question him about the obvious falsehood as soon as he found a chance.

Something told him there was more to her story, that she was in some sort of danger, but it still bothered him that she'd seen fit to lie. It implied a lack of trust. He sat in a chair next to her, at the outer edge of the circle. His disability aggravated him—he wished to hold her hand, but she was on his left side. If only he could offer her that simple comfort.

Constance said, "Anna, you made mention of your misfortunes. Rose was nearly captured and sold by this horrific group. Did you go through something similar?"

Anna reached for her husband's hand, as if to draw strength from the man seated beside her. "My sire, Lorne MacGruder, tried to keep me prisoner because he did not wish for me to wed David. He was so intent on preventing our wedding, he drugged me, hid me, and attempted to marry me to an old man. When his attempts to keep me away from David failed, my brother sold me to men who work in the Channel of Dubh. I could have easily been sent across the seas. 'Tis why I'm especially eager for David to help his cousins."

Daniel could actually see the fear in Constance's eyes. Her eyes jerked from person to person, her hands twisting her gown in her lap. Every now and then she'd try to stop herself from fidgeting, but it would start again moments later. Aye, something had put a fright in her. Fortunately, Braden stood, reached for his wife's hand and said, "Come,

David and Anna, we'll show you to a chamber abovestairs. Then, once you're settled, we'd be happy to give you a tour of our land."

In the ensuing flurry of activity, Constance managed to duck out into the kitchens without anyone taking notice.

Except him. Daniel followed her.

She headed straight out the back door, then launched herself at a dead run for the back curtain wall.

Daniel trailed along, watching as she burst into tears and threw herself onto a bench at the back of the property. She dropped her head into her hands, bawling for all she was worth.

Daniel hesitated, but her cries nearly broke his heart. Mayhap she wished to be alone, but he couldn't find it in his heart to walk away. He tiptoed over to the bench and clasped her shoulder lightly so as not to startle her, but his touch jarred her badly enough for her to jump. She lifted her head and then threw her arms around his neck once she recognized him.

"Lass, what has you so troubled?" He sat with a flop, then managed to tug her onto his lap and enveloped her with his arms, his right hand grabbing his left forearm.

Constance lifted her head long enough to say, "Oh, Daniel. I know not where to start." Her head fell back onto his shoulder and she sobbed more, her entire body twitching and heaving every so often with a ragged breathing pattern that made him wish to go in search of the person who'd caused her to feel so wretched.

"Constance, you're trembling. It cannot be all that bad."

Her response was to lift her head, peer up at him and nod, then drop her head back down, her grip on his biceps tightening as though she'd never let go.

He rested his head on the top of hers, a position that allowed him the luxury of taking in her flowery scent, the silky strands of her hair teasing his cheek. "Does this have anything to do with your sire?"

She nodded, not lifting her head.

"Your sire isn't Glenn of Buchan, is he?"

She stiffened in his arms, then pushed against his chest to separate herself from him, moving to the end of the bench. He reached for her, but she pushed him away again, her breath still hitching, and she began that infernal twiddling of her fingers again. Now he knew how upset she was.

"Just your hand?" he whispered. "May I hold your hand, Constance? You're still my sweet bluebell, no matter what happens."

She stared at him for close to an eternity before she gave a slow nod, followed by a hiccup.

He took her hand when she offered it, set it on his lap and began to lightly trace his fingers over hers. He started at her thumb and brushed each of her fingers slowly, rhythmically. Her gaze followed his path up and down each one, and neither one of them spoke until he'd covered her entire hand.

He hoped he'd calmed her down enough for them to have a serious conversation. "Constance, you need not tell me who your true sire is, but Glenn of Buchan died in battle, and he had only two sons and a daughter. I know his daughter Davina."

She tore her gaze from his fingers, looking up at him, her face red and swollen from all the tears. "'Twas the only name I could think of."

"You need not tell me," he said. "Just answer me one question, if you will. Is your true sire the reason you're at the abbey?"

She pulled out a linen square from her sleeve and dabbed at her eyes. When she finished, she gave a deep sigh and whispered, "Aye, but 'tis all I'll say."

"Fair enough, and I'll thank you for that." His fingers traveled up her arm, continuing the light caress up her shoulder, her neck, and her cheek. She shivered, still not pushing him away, so he leaned forward, his lips touching hers in a soft caress. He pulled back and gazed into her eyes, hoping she would allow him to continue. "I care verra much for you, and I'd like to help you. 'Tis the only reason I'm here."

She whimpered and cupped his face, tugging him toward her. He kissed her again, and she parted her lips with another whimper. He teased her tongue and she matched him, tasting and touching each other until he feared he'd lose himself just from the sounds she made.

But he did not wish to take advantage of her, so he ended the kiss. She fell toward him, and he grinned, wrapping his arm around her shoulder. "I want more of you, too, lass, but not here, not now." He chuckled, kissing her forehead as she rested her head on his shoulder.

"Daniel, I know not what to do."

"If you share something about your confusion, I may be able to help you, but I cannot if you don't let me in."

She sighed, a sound filled with so much discontent and frustration that he wished to beat to a pulp whoever had made her feel such pain. Was it her sire or someone else?

"I ran away from home. Listening to Anna talk about her family upset me. I don't want to talk about my sire." She pulled something out of the folds of her gown, rubbing her fingers over the surface while she stared down at it.

"What is that you hold?" Daniel asked.

She held it out for him to see. A dark red amulet with an odd shape to it. "I took it from home. Do you see how 'tis nearly in the shape of a heart? I had to have something to remind me of my dear mother. I consider it my lucky stone."

"The gem is quite beautiful. I would advise you not to allow anyone to know you carry it. It could be quite valuable." Daniel took her hand in his again, rubbing her knuckles with his thumb. "You are old enough to make your own decisions. You need not see him again if you do not wish to. Tell me this. Are you happy at the abbey? Do you have the calling to become a nun?"

She sat up again, her chin quivering as soon as her gaze found his. "I'm not sure, but my sire hates me, so I have nowhere else to go."

Daniel had no answer at the moment. He wished to protect his wee bluebell, but would she let him? And could he offer such a thing when he'd made a commitment to seek out the wicked men who ran the Channel of Dubh?

He couldn't help but stare at the red gemstone still in her hand. Its beauty was mesmerizing, and the more he looked at it, the more certain he was of its value. He'd have to convince her to keep it hidden.

"Constance, how many people at the abbey have seen this stone?"

"I'm not sure. I keep it well hidden. 'Tis always in my pocket. Why?" She looked up at him, and the trust in her soulful green eyes humbled him.

"I would show as few people as possible. Unsavory characters lurk where you least expect them. Be verra careful with it."

They both stared at the large object, the light reflecting off the different facets of the blood-red stone.

Whoever Constance was, he knew one thing for certain. Her family was far from poor.

CHAPTER SIX

———◆———

CONSTANCE RUBBED THE SLEEP OUT of her eyes the next morning. She'd dreamt of Daniel holding her, talking sweetly to her, so vivid she'd thought it was real. The dream had almost chased away memories of her other dream, in which her sire locked her up just as Anna's sire had done to her.

Sweet Daniel had helped her forget everything.

She couldn't help but sigh at the memory of the dream and, even better, the memory of her real experience with Daniel. Daniel nuzzling her, mesmerizing her, kissing her senseless. She closed her eyes to savor the thoughts. He was nothing like any of the other lads she'd known.

Especially the one she'd fancied herself in love with.

She dashed that thought from her mind. Much as she would like to stay here, she'd decided it was impossible. Her sire's men would catch up to her eventually. They could steal her away before she was able to scream. She'd seen them in action many times before.

She would not give them that chance. There was no choice but for her to ultimately return to the abbey, though she thought she could steal a few more days of happiness. She made a bargain with God. *Three more days, Lord, and I'll return to do Your work, whatever You wish of me.*

Three more days with Daniel, please!

Then she would return to her safe haven, to the place her sire's men could never hurt her or steal her away.

She finished her ablutions with haste because she would not waste this precious time with Daniel, nor would she spend any more tears on her situation. Today was her day to enjoy this gift she had been given. She searched for something to wear, and finally knew it had to be the green gown, so she slid into it, then slowed her pace to wrangle with all the ribbons.

A knock on the door interrupted her as she ran her fingers through her long locks. She had no one to plait it for her so she'd decided to leave it unbound for the day.

"Enter," she called out, smoothing her quickly donned gown and tying up the last ribbon.

Cairstine opened the door slowly. "My apologies we have no maid to tend to your needs, but is there anything I can do to assist you? Do you need help with ribbons or plaiting your hair?"

"Nay, I have a gown with the bindings in the front."

"Oh my," Cairstine crooned. "'Tis a most lovely gown, my dear."

Constance smoothed the wrinkles out of the skirt, one of the few she'd managed to bring with her from home. Her mother had chosen the fabric and she'd worn it to a wedding. It was made of a forest green velvet with ribbons that matched the color of her hair. "Many thanks. 'Tis my best gown."

Cairstine fluffed at the folds, helping her to smooth it out. "I adore the fabric."

Steenie came barreling into the room, brimming with excitement. "Mama, Daniel plans to take Constance for a ride to the waterfall. May I go with him?"

"Did you ask Daniel?" Cairstine pivoted to speak to her excited son.

"I did. He said I could go along. He's bringing a picnic basket, too. May I go, please?"

"Steenie, remember your manners. Did you greet the lady yet?"

The laddie hopped from one foot to the other, his golden hair bouncing with each movement, though he kept his hands folded in front of him in an attempt to contain his excitement. "Greetings to you, my lady."

"You may call me Constance, Steenie. My, but you look exactly like your mama. He has the most beautiful green eyes." Constance glanced from mother to son again, enjoying the similarities.

"I'm not beautiful. I'm a lad and I'm handsome. Lasses are beautiful, not lads. I will be a warrior someday when I'm bigger. A Grant warrior."

His answer reminded her so of her brothers. How they'd hated the thought of ever being compared to a lassie. She recalled their younger days when they'd talked of going to England to be knighted. Regret seeped through her, but she shook the feeling away and smiled at her visitors. "I'm sure you'll be a mighty warrior for Clan Grant, lad, and my apologies. You most definitely are a lad and not a lass. I would love for you to join us."

Cairstine said, "Aye, you may go along, Steenie. Please go to your chamber and find some warm wool hose to wear."

"Aye, Mama." He flew back out the door with a bang, almost barging into another person outside the door. Daniel.

"They said I could go," the wee lad exclaimed. "Don't leave without me, please. I must put some hose on."

Daniel chuckled, glancing down at Steenie's bare feet. "Aye, you better get some hose and your best boots, or you'll get nettles all over and you won't be able to walk by morn."

"But will you wait?" he asked, still hopping up and down.

"Aye, I promise to wait for you, lad."

Steenie disappeared in a flash, and Daniel turned to Constance, his brilliant smile taking her breath away. How handsome he was. How had she managed to snag the attention of such a fine lad?

"I think the lad has spoiled my surprise," he said with a grin, "but could I beg you to go along with the two of us, Constance? There's a fine burn and waterfall not far from here. I'll take some nice furs to use on the rocks since there's a chill in the air."

Constance stopped herself from clapping due to her own excitement. Was Steenie's joy catching or was she just this excited from being around Daniel? "I would love to join you, Daniel."

Cairstine stepped around the two of them and said, "I'll go check on my son."

Daniel's gaze traveled from her face down to her toes. "My, but you are lovely today, lass. 'Tis a beautiful gown and it sets off your hair just right. You might think it odd I would notice such a thing, but my mother has a dash of red in her hair and she's always fussed over colors matching or clashing with her hair. She would love your gown. Believe it or not, my sire, Micheil, has always helped my mother pick out the fabric for her gowns. He had an eye for it, and he'd approve of this one for certes."

Constance blushed, "My thanks. I would love to meet your parents someday." The sentiment was true, though she knew it was not to be.

He held his hand out to her and said, "May I escort you down the stairway?"

She placed her hand in his, the warmth from his touch traveling up her arm, so inviting that she found herself leaning toward him as they walked down the wide passageway.

They were halfway down the staircase, Daniel next to the railing with his left arm now at her back, when Steenie burst around the corner and bolted down the steps, only to trip as soon as he set eyes on them. They both reached for him just as Cairstine screeched from the top of the stairs. Daniel caught him with his right hand and righted him, but not before Steenie plowed into Constance, throwing her off balance and knocking her down the stairs.

She screamed and flailed for something to grab onto, reaching for Daniel's free left arm, but there was nothing to grasp onto because his one hand still held Steenie. Daniel did his best to stop her fall, but he had nothing to grasp her with, and lost her. Losing her balance completely, she tumbled down the rest of the stairs, skirts flying everywhere, until she landed in a heap at the base of the stairs, her head hitting the stone floor.

Lying flat on her back, she didn't move, still stunned at what had happened. Pain shot through her body from her hip to her head, from her left foot to her elbow. Tears threatened to flood her cheeks, but she refused to cry. Surely she'd shed enough tears.

Before she knew it, Steenie and Daniel were kneeling at her side.

She could hear Cairstine's voice from a distance, hitching with panic. "Steenie, see why I tell you to slow down on the staircase?"

"Mama, I'm sorry. Forgive me, Constance, I didn't mean it," he said, bursting into hot tears that splashed onto her gown. "Are you dead?"

"Nay, Steenie. I'm fine. I'll be fine in a moment, I just cannot move yet." She focused on the rafters above, trying to set her vision to rights, but she couldn't.

"God's bones, Constance." Daniel grasped her hand with his, as gentle as if she were a babe. "I'm so sorry. I tried to stop you, but I reached for Steenie first..."

The look in his eyes told her how much he cared, how sorry he was for failing to break her fall. She patted his forearm. "Daniel, you did the right thing. You needed to save the laddie first."

A big pair of arms lifted Steenie away. "Papa, I'm so sorry. I didn't mean it." He clutched Braden, who whisked him away after mumbling another quick though heartfelt apology for the accident.

Daniel continued, "What hurts? Can you sit up? Here, I'll help you."

A woman knelt on her other side. The lady was lovely, and her aura was quite unlike anything she'd ever seen. She must have hit her head quite badly because now she was seeing heavenly auras. She recognized the woman as Braden's mother only when her gaze landed on Brodie, Braden's sire. "Lass, stay still until you know what hurts. You don't want to make it worse. My name is Celestina."

"But I think I can sit up with Daniel's assistance." She clung to Daniel's forearm as though he would keep her from falling again.

"What hurts the most?" the lovely woman asked.

She did her best to slow her racing heart, paying attention to her body so she could answer the question. Gulping, she finally focused on what hurt most. "My head, my left ankle…it twisted, I think. I also have smaller pains, in my elbow and my hip."

"Those will probably be naught but bruises by the morrow, but let's sit you up and see if we can get you to a chair." The woman even had the calming voice of an angel.

Constance nodded her agreement, though even that small movement pained her, while Connor brought over a chair and Daniel helped her into it, his cheeks flaring red when he struggled with his one hand.

The angel pulled up a stool and sat next to her. "May I look at the back of your head? There's a bit of blood on the floor."

"Aye," Constance managed to get out, fighting the pain that called to her from so many places. "Thank you for your assistance. You look like an angel."

Celestina smiled. "I've been called that before, but it was many years ago."

Celestina's hands palpated the back of her head, her touch quite tender. "Aye, you have a cut back there and a big bump. I'm sure you'll have quite a headache. I have a potion I can give you to ease your pain."

"Please do not put me to sleep."

"All right, my dear. I'll prepare a light mixture for you once I finish dressing your wounds."

Cairstine brought over linen strips and a basin of water, setting them on a nearby table. "Constance, I'm so sorry," she said, her lips twisting with worry. "Steenie acts before he thinks. He was so excited about going with you and Daniel."

"He was just being a little boy. 'Twas no one's fault."

Everyone else hovered around trying to help, but her vision remained blurry so she closed her eyes while Celestina cleaned her wound. Once the older woman finished her ministrations, Constance whispered, "My thanks to you. Daniel, will you help me stand, please? I wish to see how bad my ankle is."

Daniel said, "Of course. David," he said to his brother, who stood outside her field of vision, "grab her other elbow please?"

The two helped her to stand, but excruciating pain shot through her left ankle as soon as she put weight on it. She fell back into the chair. "I think I broke my ankle."

Celestina lifted her foot and set it on a nearby chair, arranging it so Constance could see her ankle. She motioned to all the men surrounding them. "Go away and allow me the chance to examine her. I've spent enough time with our family healers to judge broken bones."

The men all turned their backs and moved toward the hearth while Celestina lifted Constance's skirt and set it above her knee. "I'm afraid it is quite swollen, Constance," she said softly. "I'll just push on it a bit to see if I can feel a broken bone."

Constance hissed when she touched one spot, and then another and another. They all hurt.

"I think you turned your ankle," Celestina said. "You must not walk on it much. I also suggest you sit as you

are for a bit, with your foot up on a stool. It may help
the swelling go down. I recall Brodie's sister Brenna saying
'twas important, and she's one of the finest healers in all
the land."

"Please do not worry yourself about me," Constance said,
feeling guilty for all the fuss she'd caused. "I'll manage."

The beautiful woman said, "I do care about you, we
all do, even though we've just met." She reached up and
brushed back some stray hairs that had fallen into Constance's face.

"Have you always lived here?" Constance felt compelled
to ask. "You sound like you have an English accent." Her
mother had the same musical lilt to her voice.

"We lived at Clan Grant for a long time. But the man
who raised me was a baron brought from England to Scotland. I didn't speak Scots for a while. Much as I try to
eliminate the accent from my speech, it still remains. My
heart is Scottish."

Constance felt a bolt of panic, and bile rose in the back
of her throat. "What barony was that man? And was he not
your father?"

"It's a long story, but I was raised by Baron Lunde, though
he's now passed on. He was not my true sire." Celestina
reached for the linen strips and began her work. "I'll place
a small bandage on your head, then I'll wrap your ankle to
see if that helps ease your pain."

Constance's fear increased fourfold. Barons were always
aware of other barons. Even though Baron Lunde had
passed on, it was still possible...

Could this woman know her father?

CHAPTER SEVEN

THE NEXT DAY, DANIEL CARRIED Constance outside, determined to have their picnic as planned. Steenie followed them, carrying the basket, babbling as he often did.

Daniel found a nice spot under a shade tree and gave Steenie instructions. Reaching into the top of the basket, the lad retrieved the furs and set them on the ground. Daniel settled Constance on the soft furs, immediately afraid he'd hurt her when she winced.

"Is it your head? Your ankle?"

"My headache. But do not worry, Celestina mixed another potion for me. I would still like to have our picnic. I'm hoping this will make me forget all about my head."

Steenie set the basket down, then his eyes darted toward the stables. Brodie was heading inside. "Grandpapa, wait for me," he cried out. Then he took off without another thought.

Daniel called out to the running lad, "No picnic, Steenie?"

"Nay, 'tis no waterfall."

Constance smiled at the boy's logic. "He is a sweet lad, and he felt awful about the accident."

Daniel couldn't help but chastise himself over the accident. If he'd only had two hands, he could have grabbed both of them. His insufficiency had caused her pain.

"My apologies again for not grabbing you. I should have

grabbed you first."

Daniel emptied the basket contents onto the clean plaid he'd set down near the furs, then settled near Constance with a frustrated sigh.

She set her hand on his forearm. "Nay, you should not have. The lad was more important."

"I disagree. The lad is flexible. He would have rolled to the bottom and gotten up and run out the door two seconds later, as quickly as he just left us." He glanced toward the stable. "Young lads are resilient."

"Unless he hit his head. I agree that lad's bones are more flexible. When I think of all the…" she froze, but then continued, "…tumbles my brothers took without injury to their bones, I'd have to agree with you, but a head injury could have been serious. Daniel, you did the right thing. I have a couple of bruises, but everything will heal."

Daniel wished to tell her that he would have moved heaven and earth to save her, and that his lack of two hands shamed and encumbered him, but he could not find the words. He settled for something close to the truth. "Bluebell, you know I would have done anything to save you. I feel as though I failed you." His gaze caught hers, and he saw nothing there but pain and sympathy.

Or was it pity? He hated pity.

She reached up and set her fingers to his lips. "Daniel, nay. If I've learned anything in my short life, it's that we cannot undo something that happened. We must deal with it. I'm so sorry you lost your hand, but it doesn't change who you are. I care verra deeply for you, but it has to do with your heart, not your hand. And we cannot undo my fall. Please stop worrying yourself about it."

But he couldn't. It was that simple. He'd never get that image out of his mind. Constance flailing, reaching for him when he wasn't there for her, her eyes flooding with fear.

What if he let her down again?

She reached for his chin, lifting his gaze to hers. "Daniel? Promise me you'll stop blaming yourself?"

"I cannot promise, but I'll try."

She leaned forward and pressed her lips against his, a soft, tender kiss that ripped at his insides because of how genuine he knew it to be. She meant what she'd said.

Now, why couldn't he do as she asked?

Hellfire, but he feared he really was in love with the lass. Unfortunately, he didn't deserve her.

———◆———

ABOUT AN HOUR LATER, THEY'D finished their food. Constance couldn't stop giggling at a tale Daniel had told her about Clan Ramsay, his sire's clan. They sounded so warm and loving, but full of trickery and teasing at the same time.

"I cannot wait to meet your uncle Logan."

"And don't forget Aunt Gwyneth."

Constance blushed and whispered, "She has quite a reputation, does she not?"

A call echoed out from the stables, though she didn't recognize the voice.

"Guards! All men at the front gates!"

Fear shot through her as Daniel bolted to his feet. "Stay here," he said. "I know you cannot move, but as soon as I find out what transpires, I'll return to do what's best for you. Trust me."

He leaned over and kissed her forehead before he took off flying toward the gates. She had no idea what it meant, so she stayed where she was and listened.

And prayed. *Please do not let it be my sire's men.*

Horses were saddled and mounted, men were shouting and yanking swords out of their sheaths. What was happening?

Constance managed to shimmy her way over to the tree, then used it to pull herself up so she could see better, but she still couldn't see past the gates.

Cairstine and Anna flew out of the keep and down the steps, both shouting for Steenie, who came running. "Mama! I'm helping with the horses. Paddy wants to go outside. Should I ride him out?"

"Nay. Paddy does not belong with destriers. Over here, Steenie, until we find out what's happening."

Steenie noticed Constance and said to his mother, "We must help her."

With their assistance, she managed to hobble between Steenie and Anna. They moved her back toward the castle, and she caught sight of the gates, which had now been opened. As soon as Cairstine noticed a line of horses out front, she suggested they take cover behind the stables. The others agreed, anxious to know what was afoot.

One particular guard seemed to take charge of the others while Braden headed out of the gates. Cairstine whispered, "Thank goodness Moray finally came to assist Braden. He brought three others with him. We need guards."

Constance said, "You didn't have any before?"

"This all happened so quickly, but Braden knew Moray would be his second once he was able to bring his mother along. She stays in her cottage, but she and Aunt Fina are getting along well. She promised to help cook and she's wonderful."

Steenie burst out, "She puts honey in my porridge."

Cairstine patted his head with a smile, but her gaze returned to the activity outside their gates. They watched in silence, anxious to see what the visitors were about.

"What do they want?" Anna asked.

Steenie snuck out and said, "I'll find out." But his mother grabbed him by the collar and tugged him back.

"Nay, you will not. Your da will be furious if you go out there."

"But I wish to help," he whined.

Constance broke out into a sweat even though the temperature was quite cool. She listened as best she could, but she only caught bits and pieces.

"…looking for a lass who is lost…"

"…we'll pay good money for any lasses you don't want…"

She gasped at that comment. That meant they couldn't be searching for her. They were looking for any lass they could find.

Apparently, Cairstine had also overheard them. Her hand flew to her mouth and she whispered, "The Channel of Dubh…"

Steenie squealed and hugged his mother, burying his face in her skirts. "Don't let them take me, Mama. I'll be good. I promise!"

"No one will ever take you away from me again, Steenie," she said firmly. "We're part of Clan Grant and they will protect us. Come, we'll go inside."

They struggled a wee bit but managed to assist Constance up the steps and into the great hall. Celestina stood in front of the hearth, staring into the flames.

Steenie ran straight to her, "Grandmama, 'tis the men from the Channel of Dubh. I hope Papa kills them all."

Celestina calmed Steenie down, rubbing his back and saying, "I think we need to find a repast for the men when they come in. Will you help me in the kitchen, Steenie? Hilda will need our assistance. Mayhap Anna will join us, too."

Steenie took off toward the kitchen door at a run, followed by Anna, while Celestina turned to Constance and Cairstine and said, "'Tis not a good time to be an unmarried lass. God help all the lassies out there."

Constance kneaded her hands in her lap, doing her best not to twiddle her fingers the way she often did, while they waited for the men to return. Less than an hour later, several filed back in.

"I say we follow them," Connor said.

Brodie said, "For what? You cannot demand justice if they've not done anything yet. They'll come up with some excuse for asking after the lasses. Besides, we don't have enough men to fight them all. There were a dozen men, mayhap more elsewhere. My guess is they're headed out to search more castles and manor homes."

Moray said, "The three guards I brought with me are strong swordsman. We could assist."

Connor shook his head. "We need more men. We need Roddy, Gavin, and Gregor. Mayhap Will and Maggie. All the cousins."

As soon as Daniel came inside, he hurried over to her and wrapped his arm around her shoulders. "You did not hurt yourself coming inside? Forgive me for leaving you alone."

"Nay, I'm fine, but I'm worried about those men. Do they know I'm here? Have they seen me? Did they say anything about seeking a lass with red hair?" Her voice rose with each word.

"Nay," Daniel said. "They did not ask about you."

"But they could. Daniel, I need to go back to the abbey." No matter how she tried, she couldn't stop glancing at the doorway every few seconds, knowing at any time someone could come inside looking for her.

Men paid by her sire. Or perhaps the men who'd just left, another group who'd put her on a galley ship much like the one in which Rose and Euphemie and Ada had been held captive, full of sweating and spitting, bullying beasts. Rutting bastards. Wasn't that a term she'd heard once?

How was she to survive this impending doom ready to drop down on her at any moment? She had to go back where it was safe.

"Daniel? Please?"

"Now? I'll not take you out there while there's a dozen men on horseback looking for lasses. 'Twould be foolish."

She wiped the sweat from her brow, knowing he was

right. "On the morrow. Promise me you'll take me back on the morrow." She chewed on her bottom lip as she awaited his answer. "Please?"

Daniel gave her an odd look, but then said, "We'll take you back at first light. Then the rest of us will head south."

She breathed a sigh of relief. She refused to bring harm to these people, who'd shown her naught but kindness. Though part of her wished to unburden herself to Daniel, she must keep her secret.

CHAPTER EIGHT

———————

DANIEL DIDN'T KNOW WHAT TO think. Constance had managed to grab a piece of his heart, but now she wished to return to the abbey. She wished to leave him.

The lasses had all gone to bed and he sat in a chair by the hearth, drinking an ale with Connor and Braden. Neither of them asked him about Constance, but he knew his respite was over when David came down the stairs, grabbed an ale, and joined them. He did not wait long before he went after Daniel.

"I've not seen you have any kind of relationship with a lass before, Daniel. Do you wish to tell me more?"

Braden grinned. "How many summers are you, Ghost?"

"I'm nearly ten and eight. Old enough to like lasses. Plenty old enough to marry should I choose to do so."

His brother just quirked his brow at him before he took another swig of his ale. "Have you found out who she really is?"

Daniel rested his elbows on his knees, staring into the fire. "Nay. She admitted to lying about Buchan but said that she couldn't tell me what her real name was."

Connor gave a low whistle. "She told you her sire was Glenn of Buchan? She surely is hiding from something."

"Or someone," Braden said. "Is that why she panicked when the men came today?"

"'Tis probably the reason she wishes to head back to the abbey on the morrow," David said.

Daniel sat back and looked at them. "I cannot answer everything. I don't know why she lied, but I can tell you that she fears her sire, whomever he is. I had hoped she'd have the chance to relax here, enough to tell me more, but instead, her fears appear to have worsened. Between the fall, the pain she's in, and the men at the gates looking for lasses, she's on edge. If we wish to go after those men, mayhap 'tis best if I honor her wishes and return to the abbey right away. I do think we ought to follow the bastards."

"Daniel," David said. "'Twasn't your fault she fell down the stairs. I know your mind."

"I agree," Braden said. And Connor nodded.

"Nay?" He bolted out of his chair. "I grabbed for her with my left arm. She tried to grab onto me, but there was naught for her to clasp. It *was* my fault. True, Steenie lost his balance, but I should have been able to stop her fall. You all think she's heading back to the abbey because of the men on horseback? I don't. 'Tis an easy excuse, but I believe she's thought better of accepting my suit."

Connor shook his head. "She clearly has feelings for you. She came here because of you. Why else would she have accepted your invitation but not Rose's?"

Daniel forced himself to sit down again and played with the edge of his goblet as he stared at it. "I'll tell you why she's leaving. Because I can't protect her. What is a Highlander supposed to do but protect the innocent? And I failed her in that." He dropped his hand from the goblet and passed his gaze from one cousin to the next, ending with his brother. "What have our sires all taught us since we were out of the cradle? Protect the innocent. Protect those who cannot help themselves. I did a pish poor job of it, did I not?"

David shook his head adamantly, leaning toward him. "You are not thinking clearly, Daniel. I know you're young, but if you've found someone you have strong feelings for, you need to pursue her before you lose her. Has my experience with Anna taught you naught?"

Daniel did his best to keep his voice level, but he failed. "If she doesn't reciprocate those feelings, what is the point? Besides, for now, I'm needed in the Band of Cousins. As soon as I take her back to the abbey, I'm going to head to Ramsay land, look for Gavin and Gregor. We need to stop those men. Forget I ever mentioned her. We're not right for each other. Connor, will you travel with me?"

"Aye," he said in his usual calm tone. "But you should have a serious discussion with Constance before you go. If you have any feelings for her, you should tell her before she takes her vows, but more importantly, you need to find out what she's afraid of and why. Else you might go back for her, only to learn she's gone—and you can't find her because you don't even know her true name."

Daniel glared at his cousin, irritated with everyone for telling him what to do. He was also irritated that Connor had thought of something he hadn't. "Connor, why should I take your advice when you're not married? What do you know about lasses?"

Connor locked his gaze on Daniel's and said, "Mayhap I don't know much, but there's one thing I do know. When I find the lass I wish to marry, I'll never let her go. I want a marriage like my parents', and I'll settle for naught less. If I must wait, I will. But when I find her, she'll never get rid of me."

"Daniel, you need to stop thinking your missing hand is causing your problems. It isn't. It's your head that's misleading you," David said. "Don't do something you'll regret."

Daniel said nothing. What could he say? He wouldn't let on how strong his feelings were for Constance because they'd spend another hour trying to convince him to marry her. But how could he build toward a future with a lass who didn't trust him enough to tell him her sire's name?

But worse than that, she didn't trust him to protect her.

He could see it in her eyes.

Without trust, they were nothing together.

————◆————

As soon as Constance arrived back at the abbey, she went directly to her chamber and cried her eyes out. Rose was gone and so was Daniel. She'd probably never see him again. She'd slept late, because it had taken so long for her to fall asleep, and when she'd awakened, the group of guards and cousins was ready to travel. She'd barely had the chance to say goodbye to Cairstine and Anne and Celestina. She'd hoped to get the chance to speak to Daniel alone, but the opportunity never arose. The journey had been wrought with tension, the guards all on edge every time a twig cracked, but there was also tension between the two of them. She knew she'd hurt him by holding back her true sire's name.

She just couldn't risk revealing the truth to him yet. He had to trust her on that, and the obvious truth was he didn't.

A knock sounded on her door, so she wiped her face with a linen square and sat up. "Enter," she whispered.

To her surprise, it was Ada, one of the lasses whom Daniel and his friends had saved. "What's wrong, Constance?"

Constance shrugged her shoulders, then said, "I miss Rose." It wasn't a complete falsehood because she did miss her dear. "Ada, I'm so sorry for all you endured on that galley ship."

Ada sat on the end of the bed. "When Father Seward gave me to those men, I wanted to cry, but then they gave us something that put me to sleep, so I don't recall much else. That was wise on their part. If I'd been awake during the thunderstorm on the water, I would have been screaming and heaving over the side of the boat. I don't know how Rose saved us. Some of the other lasses are jealous, but I'm happy for her."

Talking about her dear friend would only bring her tears back. It was all just too raw at the moment. "How have things been here?"

"Pretty quiet, but they're bringing some young orphans here to be cared for."

Sister Murreall appeared in the doorway. "Welcome back, my dear. The abbess would like to see you when you are ready."

"All right. I'll go see her now."

The nun nodded to her gown. "You might wish to put on your novice clothing instead, lass. There are two clean gowns and shifts in the chest."

Constance sighed and stood up. "I'll be right along as soon as I change, Sister."

"Child, are you limping? Are you hurt?"

Constance wouldn't lie about this. "I took a fall at Muir Castle and sprained my ankle, but do not worry. 'Tis much better. It only aches if I walk too much." She'd leave out the part about her headaches. Those she could manage.

"Do you need assistance?"

"Nay, I just move slowly, but my thanks, Sister Murreall."

"If you change your mind, you need only call my name. I'll hear you." The sweet woman smiled before she ushered Ada out.

The two left and Constance did her best to improve her appearance for the abbess. She washed her face after she changed, though the redness around her eyes would probably remain. She took a deep breath, said a quick prayer, and slowly padded down the passageway and the stairway until she reached the abbess's office.

Surprised to see the door open, she paused in the entryway and rapped lightly on the wood. The abbess had her back to Constance, perusing something written on parchment, but she whirled around, skirts billowing. When she saw it was Constance, her expression cleared. "Good day to you, child. Welcome back. Please sit down, Constance, but close the door first."

She did as instructed and took the chair opposite the desk. The abbess sat across from her in her usual chair.

"You miss your friend, I see. I'm assuming that's the cause of your swollen eyes?"

She nodded, sniffling a bit as she struggled to hold her tears in. Why did she have to discuss Rose?

"And Sister Murreall tells me you've sprained your ankle?"

"Aye, but 'tis much better."

"Take your time wherever you go." The mother abbess cleared her throat before she began her lecture, or what she guessed would be a lecture. "I'll not remind you of Rose, my dear, so let's move on. We've been advised that we will have a small group of bairns brought to the abbey. They are orphans of various ages ranging from two to eight summers. I was wondering if you would be willing to teach the lasses and also watch over them during meals and chapel. I'm sure they'll be quite frightened when they arrive."

Constance could feel just a wee bit of excitement over this possibility. "I would love to help with the young ones."

"That brings me to another issue I wish to discuss with you." The abbess sat forward in her chair, now leaning toward Constance with her hands folded on the desk. "Your heritage. I allowed you the chance to think about it, but now I wish for you to tell me who your sire is."

Constance stared at her fingers, a sudden panic tearing through her. What should she do? Tell the truth? She could not. If the abbess knew the truth, she would probably turn her over to her father, and she couldn't let that happen. She wished to live a normal life, or as close to normal as possible.

"Constance, only lasses born of noble blood are taught to read, and many times the nobility only teach their lads, not their lasses. Why were you taught?"

She decided the truth would not give away her identity. "My eldest brother taught me to read, so my parents asked me to teach the others. My sisters were allowed to watch from the back of the chamber."

"My thanks to you. I believe you tell the truth. It makes me proud to see lasses who are not afraid to use their minds. And since I believe in lasses learning to read along with lads, I'll ask you to teach the older bairns their letters."

She clasped her hands together and smiled. "Many thanks, Mother Abbess. I will not let you down. I promise to work verra hard."

The abbess held her hand up, indicating that Constance should stop. "I'll allow it under one condition. I need to know who your sire is."

What could she do? She wracked her brain for a solution but came up empty.

Forgive me, God, for I am about to sin. I see no other way. Please don't punish me for lying.

"Constance? What have you decided? Do you wish to work with the bairns or not?"

She tapped her feet, alternating right and left, and fiddled with her hands.

Memories assailed her in spite of herself. Her sire had always treated his guards well—until the day he had ordered one of them to be flogged in front of everyone. The man's name had been Mungo MacKenzie. So furious was her sire that he did not dare hold the whip himself, instead pacing and bellowing behind the man as he was punished for something Constance still did not fully understand. That had been the last day they'd ever seen Mungo. She only knew he'd committed an indiscretion.

The very word one of her brothers had used to describe what she herself had done.

She hadn't been allowed to watch the man's beating, but she'd snuck out to the stables with one of her brothers, peeking out of the opening between the wooden slats. The fury on her sire's face had terrified her.

"Lass, are you hearing my words?" Mother Abbess asked, leaning forward on her desk before she slapped her hand down on the wood surface, the harsh sound bringing Constance's attention back to the present.

Tears sprang to her eyes and threatened to flood her face. "I'm sorry, Mother Abbess. You ask a difficult question."

"Lass, I wish you would trust me. I'm certain I could find a way to help you, whatever troubles you believe you have. Just give me the name for now. 'Tis all I ask."

She kept her gaze down, unable to look at the woman. She had no choice but to tell another lie, and while the name she was about to give would be discovered, she could think of no others at the moment. Every other name that came to mind was certain to cause a quick response. This one she hoped could buy her time, especially since it was a total fabrication on her part, so she gulped and whispered it aloud.

"MacKenzie. My sire is Mungo MacKenzie."

CHAPTER NINE

———————

DANIEL AND CONNOR ARRIVED ON Ramsay land two days later, pleased to see Gavin and Gregor riding out to greet them.

"Why are you here and not off with your sister, Gavin?" Daniel asked.

"Maggie and Will have gone to the royal castle to deal with Jean MacDole and her accomplices. Papa went with them. Once they return, we'll decide where to go next."

Jean was Rose's mother—an awful woman who'd schemed with Father Seward to sell lasses through the Channel of Dubh.

"Aye," Connor said. "We stopped at Will's place, but his grandsire said they haven't been there in a while. You were next on our list. I haven't been here in a while. Is Torrian here?"

"Aye, he, Cailean, and Kyle are in the lists if you wish to go."

"Nay," Connor replied. "I'm off to the keep. Aunt Brenna has the best cook. I need to eat before I start sparring."

"And mayhap Jennet will be there," Daniel said, smiling. His wee cousin made him laugh like none other. She had a mighty mind, stronger than most adults, though she didn't have a strong sense of social niceties. Jennet would shock everyone and not have a care about it. She'd been kidnapped before—and had even frightened her kidnappers.

"Aye, she's eager to see you," Gregor said, giving him a

significant look. Jennet was his wee sister, though the two did not seem much alike. "Wait until you see what she's been working on. You must be a favorite of hers, Daniel." He flicked the reins of his horse and led the way across the small bridge leading to the open gate in their curtain wall.

Daniel had no idea what Gregor alluded to, but he looked forward to finding out. He lifted his face to the light wind, breathing in the hint of Scottish pine always in the air, something he loved. Once they entered the bailey, the aroma of flowers greeted him, and that reminded him of someone he was doing his best to forget.

But he couldn't forget her, not even for a moment. Already he missed Constance.

The others were talking, Gavin's voice audible above the others, but he found he couldn't pay attention. He rode along in his own world, thinking of Constance's red curls and the way she'd looked at him before he left her at the abbey, a mix of sadness and regret in her eyes, when Gavin cried out, "Do my eyes deceive me or do I see some lovesickness on your face, Daniel?" The next thing he did shocked Daniel. Gavin tipped his head back and let out his best combination of a Ramsay, Grant, Drummond war whoop.

Connor guffawed. "What the hell was that?"

Gavin laughed. "That was a *love* whoop. Daniel's got the love whoops. We all saw him with Constance."

Connor couldn't stop himself and broke into a full belly laugh. "Gavin, you're not wrong, but you better run when you dismount."

The three cousins laughed as they approached the stables. They hopped down before Daniel, who took his time. When he finally dismounted, he marched past the three of them, whose shoulders were still shaking with laughter. He stopped next to Gavin and said, "Sad to see you're so jealous." He patted Gavin's shoulder and said, "Mayhap someday, wee laddie."

A horrified look stole over Gavin's face, as if Daniel had cursed him, but the other two let out a loud, satisfied whoop.

The door to the great hall flew open and Aunt Brenna stepped out. "Are those two of my favorite nephews? If so, you better hurry up for a hug or I'll tell Cook you aren't hungry."

Daniel loved his aunt Brenna, Gregor's mother, the best healer in all the land. She'd married his uncle after curing his two bairns of a strange illness. She'd acted as mother to Lily and Torrian ever since, and they'd rarely been ill.

He left his cousins to their jests and hurried up the steps to greet his aunt. Connor let out a final laugh and climbed up after him. "Greetings to you, Auntie." He hugged her and stepped back so his cousin could do the same.

"Daniel, you look more and more like your father every day, and Connor… Oh my, you look so much like your father I find it haunting. And will you ever stop growing? Are you as tall as your sire yet?"

"I think I'm a wee bit taller, Aunt Brenna. He won't allow me to stand next to him anymore."

She chuckled. "Oh, 'tis definitely a sign you're taller. He doesn't like to be bested in anything, though he would prefer to be surpassed by one of his sons than a stranger. Come inside. I'll find you some stew and mayhap a pastry or two."

It wasn't a normal mealtime, so the hall was largely deserted, but the four cousins sat down at one of the trestle tables and ate, sharing tales of their travels, boasting about their strengths as they often did, and discussing what had happened at Braden's castle. Daniel had just refilled his goblet with ale when two voices carried across the balcony.

"Daniel! Connor!" Jennet and Brigid flew down the stairs to greet them, together as usual. They were as inseparable as their brothers, Gregor and Gavin, were.

After greeting the lads, Jennet and Brigid sat at the table

with them, waiting for them to finish their meal. Jennet seemed rather impatient, and when Aunt Brenna emerged from the kitchens, she jumped to her feet and said, "May I, Mama?"

"Of course. Now would be a wonderful time to show him your creation." Aunt Brenna came up behind Daniel and set her hands on his shoulders. "Daniel, do you recall the last time you visited, and Jennet expressed her concern about your plight of only having one hand?"

"Aye." Her questions had impressed him, demonstrating a wisdom rarely seen in a young lass of only ten summers. She'd asked him about the feeling in his arm, his shoulder, even in his missing fingers. She was a most curious lass.

"Go ahead, Jennet. Fetch it and show it to Daniel," Aunt Brenna said.

Daniel had no idea what she referred to, but he was definitely curious.

Aunt Brenna said, "Daniel, she was so taken by the seriousness of your situation, losing your hand and, more importantly, your fingers, that she set a goal for herself. We've heard of armorers attaching hooks to limbs, but we wanted to be more creative. She designed something she hopes will be helpful to you."

Now Daniel's interest was definitely piqued. The Drummond healer had suggested that he put a hook on the end of his arm, but he hadn't wished to look any more outlandish than he already did.

Jennet had disappeared into Aunt Brenna's healing chamber. He stared at the door, trying to imagine what his wee cousin could possibly have conjured up for him. But nothing could have prepared him for what Jennet carried in her hands when she rejoined them.

In fact, his cousins had started chattering on about sword fighting, but all conversation came to a halt as soon as she returned to the great hall.

Daniel was so stunned, he found himself standing, never

taking his eyes off the lass and what she carried in her arms. She set the contraption she carried on the table beside him.

"Allow me to explain, Daniel," she said in a serious tone. "After discussing this with my mama and papa, I concluded that what you need most is something to grip with, and that it was important for it be the same length as your other arm. I may have to make some adjustments," she said as she picked up her creation. "But I do believe this could assist you with a few of the most basic tasks in your life." She turned it over to show him.

He picked up the leather sleeve she'd created, presumably to slip onto his forearm and act like a new hand. As he stared at it, he did something he hadn't done in years, and he didn't care. Tears formed on his lashes, and he let them fall, only bothering to swipe them away when they interfered with his vision.

"Why do you cry, Daniel?" Jennet asked, clearly puzzled. "I did not mean to make you sad."

"I'm not sad, lass. I'm grateful," he said, finally grinning. "Go on. I wish to hear all about it."

His aunt put her arm around Jennet. "Those are tears of joy. He appreciates what you've done for him."

Brigid glanced up at Daniel, grinning at him. "I helped put it together, too. Though Jennet did all of the planning."

"My thanks to both of you."

"If you hold your arm out, I will demonstrate," Jennet said.

Daniel did as she asked, and she slipped the leather device over his forearm. "Now, my mother and I and Brigid all thought it would work best if we could tie it over your shoulder like so." She tried to tie it, but her mother stepped in to adjust it.

"Daniel, this may require some further adjustment, but you can try it and tell us how you think it works. Go ahead, Jennet, and explain the rest."

The wee lass pulled something out of the end of the odd appendage. "I had the blacksmith assist me with this. These are the parts you can extend if you wish it to pick something up. See?" She moved the metal parts in a demonstration. "If you pull on this lever, these pieces will move outward so you can grasp something with it."

"But I cannot pull with my stump, Jennet," he explained.

"Of course not. I misspoke. If you push on the lever, it should work. You can feel and push with the stump, can you not?"

"Aye, I can." Hope soared in his heart.

Aunt Brenna stepped forward. "Why don't you try it for yourself, Daniel? I can hold it, if you like."

"Aye, I'd like to try."

His cousins formed a circle around him and watched as he maneuvered Jennet's creation, wiggling and adjusting it. Eventually, he was able to push the lever, sending the metal pieces out toward a linen on the table. When they deftly grabbed the fabric, everyone erupted with applause, clapping both him and Jennet on the back.

And he stood there and cried like a lass. "Jennet, I don't know how to thank you."

"And me, too," Brigid said.

"And you, too, Brigid." He gave them each a hug and hugged Aunt Brenna, as well.

Jennet said, "If you don't mind, I'd like to watch you use it so I can make any adjustments you may need, whether to the fabric inside, the leather, or the metal. The blacksmith has agreed to adjust it as needed for you."

Daniel stopped his tears and said, "I'd be honored to have you come with me."

How he wished Constance were here to see Jennet's invention.

Maybe there was hope for them yet.

CHAPTER TEN

———•———

CONSTANCE SAT IN THE MAKESHIFT nursery surrounded by wee lasses. There were no lads in the group, to her surprise, but she thought perhaps that was for the best. She was working with two of the eldest lasses, teaching them the letters of the alphabet, and they were doing well.

At the end of the lesson, she headed over to the other part of the large chamber, joining in a game with the younger ones.

A wee lass came over and leaned against Constance's leg. "Constie, up, pweez?"

She was only two summers, and one leg was noticeably shorter than the other, so it was exhausting for her to walk. "Aye, Kelby." She picked up the dark-haired lass, who quickly dropped her head on Constance's shoulder.

"I tired," she murmured, sticking her thumb in her mouth. "I go see Mama?"

"Nay, we cannot see your mama. She's gone to heaven, lass." It had pained Constance to learn of the circumstances that had brought some of the children here. Kelby's mother had died giving birth to a younger brother, though the lad had lived. The father had decided to keep the lad and give the lass away, simply because she "wasn't like the rest."

Couldn't he see that it wasn't Kelby's fault that one leg was shorter than the other? She still worked as hard as any other lass. She practiced and practiced, but her gait had a hitch to it and she often fell down. But her efforts to simply walk were much more exhausting for her. The lass closed her eyes and Constance hummed a tune to her. The sweet bairn had quickly stolen a piece of her heart.

Kelby had come to Constance as soon as she'd seen her walk. "You same as Kebby?"

Constance hadn't known what she meant, but then when she walked over to pick the wee lass up, Kelby had pointed to her foot and said, "You walk like Kebby." Indeed, she did walk much like the girl with the strange gait.

Mother Abbess strolled inside. "All is well with the bairns. Ada?"

Ada nodded. She too had been asked to help care for the children.

The abbess continued on over to Constance's spot. "Kelby is quite taken with you, Constance. You've done a fine job with the wee ones today."

"My thanks, Mother Abbess." She was trying her best to work hard, to love the bairns, and to forget about Daniel and Rose. It was a constant struggle but keeping busy did make it easier.

"I have such hopes for you, yet you continue to disappoint me." The abbess crossed her arms and stared at the other children, her gaze not meeting Constance's.

"I…I don't understand." What had she done now? She'd done everything she could in the past few days to help the abbess and keep a smile on her face.

She'd tried so hard to forget the man she'd fallen in love with.

She just stared at the abbess, waiting for the bad news.

"You said your sire was Mungo MacKenzie?"

Now she knew she was in big trouble. "Aye," she squeaked.

"There is no Mungo MacKenzie who could be your sire. You fabricated that name, lass."

Constance dropped her gaze and closed her eyes, trying

to focus on the sweet breath of the child sleeping on her shoulder so she would not panic.

"There is a Mungo MacKenzie south of here, but he has no bairns."

Caught again. Aye, she hadn't expected this response, but she was not surprised that he'd been sent away by her sire and moved far away.

"Mayhap 'tis time for you to go to the punishment cell."

Constance couldn't argue this time, so she kissed Kelby's forehead just to give her a small consolation for the time she'd be away from her.

So be it.

———◆———

DANIEL TUGGED ON HIS NEW hand, making sure it held in place, then stepped back into the clearing they'd been using to practice not far from the lists, listening to his cousins hollering at him and his opponent as they began to face off. Daniel had always focused on making himself stronger, believing he had to work harder to take on a man with two hands, and his work had paid off. His muscle mass seemed an even match for the brawn of Cailean MacAdam, the man who'd married Gavin's sister Sorcha.

"Cailean, he's going to take you out," Connor yelled. "Go after him, Daniel. You can put him down. You'll become the *treun*, the champion of all."

Daniel had become quite fond of his new hand over the past week. His cousins had helped him train with it, culminating in this fight. Cailean MacAdam was deemed to be the toughest opponent with his bare fists.

Will and Maggie had joined them last night, talking about new leads they had on the Channel of Dubh. Due to the hard work of the Band of Cousins, the underground network had gone even farther underground.

Instead of stealing brides as was often done in the past,

reivers stole the lasses just to sell them. They awaited the return of Uncle Logan from Edinburgh before they made a new plan.

Now that Daniel could fight, he was determined to dive into this battle and do his best to win it.

Daniel rubbed his eye and spat. He already had one swollen eye thanks to Connor, and many bruises from the others. This was his first battle against Cailean. They had a gentleman's agreement not to punch in the kidneys or the groin. Aunt Brenna had insisted.

As they circled, Daniel caught sight of a couple of new attendees out of the corner of his good eye—Uncle Logan.

And his sire.

"Papa?" he asked, his fist still raised in front of his face to protect himself.

"Daniel? You're fighting with your fist? Where is your sword? And what the devil is that thing on your other arm?"

"Papa, I'm fine. I just need practice." He continued to face Cailean, dodging his swings and maneuvering around him in the small area.

Uncle Logan was two steps behind his sire. "What the hell is this? I didn't expect to find you two in the lists. I need all the men I can get to fight this battle against the Channel of Dubh. I don't need you killing each other. MacAdam, step aside." Cailean MacAdam respected his wife's father, mostly because Logan scared the hell out of him. He took a step back and held his hands in the air.

Daniel stopped to face his uncle and shouted, "Nay, Uncle Logan. I need this."

Cailean hadn't moved yet, but he also hadn't resumed the fight.

"Why, Daniel?" his sire asked.

Daniel held his new extension up for both of them to see. "I'm practicing with Jennet's contraption. I need to be able to defend myself."

"What is that?" his sire asked.

"My *treun*." He glanced over at Connor and winked at him. He'd liked that suggestion. "The secret weapon that will help make me a champion." The Gaelic word for champion was exactly what he needed. He'd call the contraption *Treun*.

Uncle Logan moved closer to take a better look at it. "Brigie told me they were working on it. Are you able to stabilize it?" he asked, putting his hand out to feel it before giving it a good yank.

His father's brow furrowed. "Jennet and Brigid did this for you?"

"With Aunt Brenna's help," he replied. "I'm not swinging with it because of the metal bits inside, but I am trying to learn to use it to defend myself. Some of these men we face are ruthless."

Uncle Logan glanced at Daniel's sire, who gave him a slight nod, then pursed his lips and said, "I'll not stop you then, but remember, your enemy also has something new to grab on to."

"Understood. Cailean, you take first shot." Daniel stepped back into the clearing, easily dodging Cailean's first swing.

"He's a brute, Daniel, but he's not quick on his feet. You can take him," Uncle Logan shouted, grinning at his son-in-law. Uncle Logan loved to taunt the lad, though he was clearly quite fond of him.

"Don't go easy on me," Daniel pressed. "I need to learn how to fight with both arms, Cailean."

The two battled for a quarter of an hour before Will finally shouted, "I declare a tie."

Daniel fell back with a smile. He hadn't bested the Ramsay warrior, but he'd held his own. He clasped Cailean's shoulder and said, "My thanks."

Daniel felt as though he'd been given a new life. Every night, he thought of all the new things he'd be able to do now that he had two hands. The grasping mechanism was still clumsy, but he'd learned how to hold a shield with the pressure from his arm, just because he had that wee bit of extension. He'd also been working with Maggie and Will on holding an arrow in place, and while he'd gained some ground, he couldn't stabilize the bow enough to shoot straight.

He knew these things took practice, but it gave him hope—hope that he might be seen as a normal man instead of a cripple. He hated how his missing hand was the first thing people noticed about him. Not his laugh or his dark hair or his muscular build, but his missing appendage.

With *Treun*, it wasn't so noticeable. It looked like his hand was stuck inside the sleeve.

Almost normal.

After the fight, Uncle Logan came up and patted him on the back. "Well done. I'm sure your sire is as pleased with that performance as I am."

"Papa? What say you about my new attachment?" He wiped the sweat off his brow with his sleeve.

"Allow me to look at it again, please?" his sire asked quietly, his eyes on *Treun*.

Daniel brought it over to him, demonstrating the mechanism inside that allowed him to grip. "'Tis still quite clumsy, and I'm raw in spots from the rubbing, but Aunt Brenna and Jennet have been adjusting it every day."

"I'll be sure to thank the lasses. I hope you can continue to make it work, Daniel. Your mother and brother will be pleased." He nodded to Logan and turned around to head back to the keep—but not before Daniel saw the tears in his eyes.

"Aye. Now that I've seen you in action, I have a proposal for the Band of Cousins. Will and Maggie will be here in a moment. Gather around," Uncle Logan said. "Cailean, go clean up. Your place is with my daughter."

Once the big man departed, Gavin, Gregor, Will, Maggie, and Daniel fell in around Uncle Logan, waiting for him to speak. "The king, while still in mourning, is even more intent on discovering who's in charge of the network, especially since so many of our young people have been jeopardized by it. He wants us to go underground, pretend to be interested in buying or selling lasses, see what we can find out."

"All of us?" Maggie asked.

"Nay, I doubt you'll be successful in this mission, Maggie. We haven't learned of any females who are involved. I also fear Will's reputation will give away his identity. I think it should be the four of you. Gavin, Gregor, Connor and now Daniel. I think you can all fend for yourselves and one another. I'm sending you out on the morrow, so rest up. You've trained enough. You need to be in top shape for this. I have no idea what you'll find."

Daniel glanced at the other three, and he could tell from the look of them they were agreeable.

"You'll all do it?"

Four heads nodded.

Daniel finally had a purpose.

CHAPTER ELEVEN

CONSTANCE PULLED OUT THE BIBLE, wishing the light was better so she could read, but just holding it close comforted her. She sat in her own cubby, locked in with a chamber pot, a Bible, and an urn of water to keep her company. The abbess came to visit her on a daily basis, asking her for the truth, but she would not budge. She guessed this prison was likely better than whatever her sire would do to punish her if she were to return home.

While she loved her sire, he was a firm believer in right and wrong. And if you were wrong, you would pay as befitted your crime. He'd done a fine job of instilling a fear of punishment in Constance and her siblings, especially after his public flogging of Mungo. Up to that point, she'd never believed all her brothers' tales of the beatings they'd endured for misbehaving, but after that, she'd changed her mind. She'd feared the price of breaking rules too much to challenge her sire.

Until that fateful day.

She shook her shoulders, swearing not to think on it again.

They fed her twice a day, so conditions were not so bad. Ada had snuck down one night to speak with her, giving her a wee bit of support and also a piece of fruit, but Constance had begged her not to risk getting herself into trouble.

She missed the bairns, especially Kelby, but she missed

Daniel more. Memories of his soft lips and tender touch kept her going, though she knew she'd probably never see him again. What had she been thinking to ever consider him as a suitor? She wasn't worthy of him.

She knew the mother abbess. She could be ruthless and relentless. Eventually, she would discover the truth about Constance's sire on her own. When she sent for him, which she most certainly would do, Constance would be whisked away to a new prison. Why hadn't she told Daniel why it was paramount for her to stay hidden? She knew he thought she didn't trust him to protect her, but nothing could be further from the truth. Daniel would protect her with his life.

She didn't deserve that.

Her mind also kept darting to her dear sister Denise and her best friend, Rose. How she missed both of them. Would she ever see her sister again? Tears misted on her lashes again, though she tried to squeeze them away. Crying would not help.

Something caught her ear. Loud banging on a door upstairs carried down to the cellars. She was the only one being punished at the moment, so she was left alone with her panic. Standing up from her pallet, she moved over to the door to listen through the small rectangle cut into the top.

"I tell you there is no one here who looks as you describe, so take your leave now." The mother abbess was clearly upset, Constance could hear it in her tone. Her voice grew louder and louder. "Go away. Guards! Where are you?"

"We have your guards surrounded. Because you're an abbey, we'll not kill them, but I won't leave without searching the place. I want every flame-haired lass brought to me. Every last one!" The man's booming voice carried all the way down the staircase as though he were standing next to her.

"As you wish," the mother abbess said, her voice rising with every word. "Your request is for a woman fully grown. I have two flame-haired bairns under five summers, and they both cry incessantly. Is that what you wish? To take a crying bairn away from me? The Lord will make you pay. He will strike you down."

She heard a loud slap followed by a light squeal from the abbess. A male voice said, "Get them now." She heard the abbess's footsteps above her, and she prayed over and over that these evil men would not take the wee ones. What would happen if they came down into the cellars and found her?

There was a possibility that these men were not looking for her. After all, she was not the only flame-haired lass in Scotland. But what if they *were* searching for her? What if her father had hired fifty men to search all the castles and abbeys in the land? He had the coin to do so.

She pulled her mother's amulet out of her sewn-in pocket and rubbed it, hoping it would bring her luck. Rubbing it as fast as she could, she prayed for the men to leave without taking anyone.

The man said, "Search this place."

Constance panicked as she listened to the chaos unfolding above stairs. Children screamed and cried as the nuns paced back and forth and did their best to answer the men's impertinent questions. She looked around her small enclosure. Where could she hide?

It was quite dark down in the basement since there was only one window to light the entire space. Part of the punishment was the lack of light. There was only one torch and it was only lit for a few hours a day. Presently, it was out.

She straightened her pallet, took her Bible and clothing and lay flush against the door, covering herself with a worn blanket. If anyone looked in the window, they wouldn't see her. They'd have to open the door. It was the best she could do under the circumstances.

She leaned against the door as two brutes barreled down the staircase.

"It's dark down here. How the hell are we supposed to see anything?"

The other man said, "She claims there's no one down here, and I doubt she'd put any lasses down in the cellar. Take a quick look in each cubby. You start at that end, I'll start at this one."

Constance held her breath when the footsteps stopped at her window. A moment passed, then the man said, "There's no one here. This is a waste of our time." His companion cursed and the two headed back up the stairs. Constance let out her breath in a relieved whoosh, only the nightmare was far from over.

More screaming, crying, and cursing rang out from above stairs, but she could do naught. She panted from fear, doing her best to take deep breaths to slow her trembling and her racing heart.

After another quarter of an hour, the men left and she finally moved out of her hiding spot.

The only thing she knew for sure was they had English accents.

Were they her sire's men or were they searching for girls for the channel? She hadn't known any of her sire's guards to be English, but she hardly knew them all.

She hoped to never know the answer to that question, but in her heart she already knew.

————◆————

THE FOUR MEN MADE THEIR way through the dark streets of Edinburgh.

"Are you sure we're going in the right direction?" Gregor asked.

Connor nodded. "Aye. Uncle Logan said this was the best place for us to find access to the underground."

With uncharacteristic reserve, Gavin muttered, "I'm not

sure I wish to find it."

Daniel settled his hand on his black-clad hip, shifting his gaze from one inn to the next. There had to be a clue somewhere. They'd gone into three taverns without hearing a whisper about the Channel of Dubh.

"What the hell are you looking for?" Gavin asked.

"Anything that tells me an establishment is not what it appears to be. You know why they call it the underground, do you not? I would guess most of the business takes place below ground. Uncle Logan said there's plenty of wagering, and they'd want to hide that. They are probably in cellars in one of these establishments."

"Daniel has a point," Connor added, turning in a circle and looking at all the buildings in the square. "There's probably a separate entrance, mayhap even in the back. That way the blackguards won't be seen by the regular patrons. Which of the inns is largest?"

They paid Daniel no mind, each of his cousins preoccupied in assessing different buildings, so he took advantage of a perfect situation.

A boisterous crowd of drunken fools came along beside them, split into a few groups of three or four lads, bellowing loudly about "wagers." Without a word to his cousins, he fell in with the crowd, moving with them as they made their way toward one of the taverns. Just as he suspected, they ambled toward a side door instead of going in through the front. A massive guard stood by the door at the base of a set of steps, and before entering, each small group handed over a stone. The group he'd joined was so deep in their cups that he managed to join them without being noticed.

Once inside, he waited for his eyes to adjust to the darkness so he could determine what he'd stumbled into. He moved over to a long counter, observing the attendant as he sold drinks and took wagers. The crowd was three deep, so no one paid any attention to him, but he couldn't help but wonder.

Wagers on what?

He followed two young men down the hall, sauntering as if he belonged there, and discovered the attraction.

Fights. Men were brawling against each other with their fists.

That answered his question. He stayed put until a few men headed out of the cellar, grumbling about their losses. Just as before, he fell in with them—far enough away that they wouldn't notice but not so far anyone else would realize he was alone—and made his way back to his confused cousins. They hadn't moved much from their position in the middle of the street.

"What the hell, Ghost? Where did you go?" Connor shouted.

Gavin chuckled but said, "I wish I knew how you did it. I turned around and you were gone. Way to prove your name."

Gregor said, "What exactly did you learn?"

"Exactly what I thought I'd find. Brutes fighting with their fists in a large chamber in the cellar of a tavern. Men were wagering coin on the outcome. You need a special stone to get inside."

Connor drawled, "Truly? Then how did you get in?"

Daniel couldn't stop the grin from covering his face. "I have my ways of sneaking about unnoticed."

"Which one?" Gavin asked.

Daniel pointed to the tavern not far ahead of them.

Gregor whistled. "The Hound and the Stag is one of the largest inns in the city," he said, waving toward the building. "Draws many after hunting. Shall we go inside for a small repast?"

"Mayhap we can find out how to get one of those stones," Gavin said.

Daniel and Connor had already taken steps in that direction. The four of them, all dressed in black, did stand out in the crowd. It was nearly midnight, and while there wasn't much pushing and shoving on the street, there were plenty of intoxicated revelers.

"If we don't find what we're looking for in any of the inns, the other possibility might be a brothel," Connor said. "They could meet in the cellar there. Though the fights might not have anything to do with the Channel of Dubh."

Gavin snorted. "I don't wish to ever see the cellars of a brothel. What they do there is not fit for my eyes."

Connor coughed.

Daniel stopped and said, "This is the one."

"How did you get into the cellar?" Gregor asked.

He tipped his head. "Side entrance at the bottom of the stairs. Can't be seen from the street at night. Let's go in through the main entrance first. See what we can learn about being allowed into the basement."

Daniel strode into the tavern and found a table in the back corner. The others followed him in, and once they were settled in, Daniel ordered four ales and tossed a coin to the lass when she served them. She tipped her ample and clearly visible bosom toward Connor, which made the other three snicker.

Connor smiled and said, "Mayhap later, lass."

Gavin waited until she left, then whispered, "Why did you tell her that? You won't sample her. I know you, Grant."

Connor shrugged. "She left with a smile, did she not? 'Tis all you need to know."

Daniel said, "You're the one who has to ask her for more information since she prefers you."

The tavern was busy—many of the patrons were standing, and most of the tables were full. Connor waited until the serving lass passed them again and said, "Lassie, may we have four meat pies and four more ales?"

"Anything for you. I like my men big," she drawled, leaning in and running her finger down his face.

"Then mayhap you'll give me some information, and I'll give you a generous tip."

"I dinnae want just the tip, I want the whole thing," she said, a husky chuckle following her words. When she finished laughing at her own joke, she said, "What is it you wish to ken?"

"We heard there was a good place to make a wager on this street. Where is it?"

She gave him a saucy look, spun on her heel, wiggling her bum at Connor, and disappeared.

When she returned, she served them a pitcher of ale and the plumpest meat pies they'd ever seen, giving Connor the largest one. She held her hand out to Connor, who paid her the necessary coin with a bit extra. Before she left the table, she tipped her other hand over his and dropped a red stone into his palm.

He gave her a puzzled look.

She whispered, "That will get you inside. Give it to the man at the side entrance and he'll let you in. Come back when you're finished." She waggled her eyebrows at him and left.

Gavin said, "Well done, Connor."

"Eat up," Daniel said. "We're going in as soon as we've finished."

"Don't eat too much, Connor," Gavin added. "You'll need your strength for later. She's got a bigger appetite than any of us." He tipped his head toward the serving lass who was still staring at them.

As soon as Connor turned his head, she winked at him and cupped her breast with her free hand.

Gregor choked.

CHAPTER TWELVE

CONSTANCE HADN'T SLEPT AT ALL. Ada had run down the stairs to check on her, tears running down her cheeks, but the abbess had called her back upstairs to help with the wee ones. Ada had quickly informed her no one was taken. She'd spent the rest of the night alone and afraid.

If those men had come looking for her, they wouldn't stop. She'd heard someone slap the abbess. They'd scared the wee lassies into tears. After giving it much thought, she knew there was only one thing to do.

She'd run away.

That was her decision, but before she could carry out her plan, she needed to do two things. First, she had to get out of the cellars. It was quite impossible for her to escape without some sort of assistance. She'd thought of asking Ada if she'd find the key and free her, but then Ada would be punished. She couldn't live with that, so her only choice in this matter was to tell the truth.

Reconciled to the fact that she had no alternative, she'd decided she would give the abbess her real name. There was another reason to do so—if Daniel ever returned for her, it would help him find her.

She could no longer deny that she loved Daniel. He was such a fine man, and he and his cousins humbled her. They worked for the good of all the Scots, trying to rid their land of the beasts who dealt in human trading. She knew he felt incomplete because of his disability, but she didn't see him that way. She didn't see him as disabled at all.

The first decision was made. The next time the mother abbess came to speak with her, she would tell her the truth.

All of it.

Then, as soon as she could, she'd run away in the middle of the night.

Which brought her to her second decision, which was more of a quandary. Where would she go? She'd come up with four possibilities.

Going home would be her last resort, something she'd only do if she were chased by nasty reivers and wild boars. The next possibility was to return to Muir Castle and hope that Daniel would be there, but she knew he and his cousins had intended to seek out more information on the Channel of Dubh. Her third choice was to return to MacDole Castle and live there by herself. While she liked that this plan did not involve anyone else, thus eliminating the worry that someone might be harmed on her account, she wasn't sure the castle would still be empty. A beautiful place like that was sure to be inhabited by now.

Her fourth choice, and the one she thought best, was to try to find Rose. To go to Grant Castle. She'd heard much about Grant land from Connor and Brodie and Celestina. It would be a long journey, but she had a general idea about which direction to go. If she could stay hidden whenever reivers were about, she could surely find some kind people in huts along the way to lead her on.

She sensed this was her best choice, and the likeliest way for her to find her way back to Daniel. If he even wanted her anymore. He'd barely spoken to her on the way back to the abbey. She knew why—he didn't think she trusted him—but once he did know the truth he would almost certainly not want her.

Footsteps echoed down the staircase.

The mother abbess made her way over to the cell, her

arms crossed in front of her.

"Did you overhear anything about the group of men who forced their way inside and held our guards hostage last eve?"

Tears slid down her cheeks as she nodded. "My apologies, Mother Abbess. I don't know who those men were. I didn't recognize any voices. They were looking for me, were they not?"

The abbess sighed deeply. "Aye, I think so. 'Tis time we stopped this charade, lass. I know not why you are hiding things from me, and I have tried to be patient with you, but I can no longer risk the well-being of so many people here. I want the truth, Constance. No more made-up tales. Who is your sire and why is he looking for you?"

"I'll tell you. May I come out, please?" Her breath hitched from her crying.

"Give me the name first, and if I deem it could be a true one, I'll allow you out so we can chat at the far table in the cellars. If you do not tell me all, I'll call a guard to place you back in the cubby and find another location for you to take your vows. I will not deal with this falsehood any longer."

Constance sobbed for a full minute before she was finally able to get control of herself.

"What do you plan to do?" the abbess said at last. "I'm wasting time standing here."

Constance continued to sob, but finally managed to get out the truth. "My parents are a baron and baroness, Douglas and Margaret Lockhart of Lee, Lanarkshire. And I do have seven brothers and sisters."

She continued to sob while the abbess unlocked the door. Without speaking, she opened it and pointed silently to the table.

Once Constance took a seat, the abbess handed her two linen squares so she could blow her nose, then sat down opposite her.

"And now you'll tell me why they're after you."

"I have two older sisters and one younger. I did learn to read on my own because my brother taught me. I learned so quickly that he asked me to teach my other brothers to read, so I became quite adept at it."

"Why are they after you? Did you run away?"

She nodded, playing with the linen square in her lap.

"Why?"

Constance swiped at her tears and stared at the far wall. She needed to answer delicately, but how? She gave up and just told the truth.

"I allowed myself to be seduced by one of the lads in the village. He lied and told me he was heir to a barony. He said he'd marry me, and we'd live in the castle up on the hill."

"Oh, child…"

"I didn't understand what he was doing until 'twas too late. I knew when I saw the blood that I was in trouble. My sire had always told me it was the only thing I had of value, so I didn't tell my parents.

"But they found out because the lad was only a stable lad in the village, and he boasted to everyone that he would soon be marrying me because he got me with child."

"But he did not? You have no belly."

"Nay. When I had my courses, my mother explained everything to me."

"So while that is indeed embarrassing, it does not tell me why you ran away."

"My sire was away when the rumors first started. When he returned, I knew I wasn't carrying, but he found out about my shameful behavior. He heard it himself in the village." She paused to wipe her eyes, recalling the look on her sire's face when he'd called her into his solar. He'd paced the room and then repeatedly hit the desk with his fist. Her mother had attempted to calm him down, but he'd ignored them both.

"My sire said he'd send me to an island by myself and leave me there. Then he promised to tie me to a pole and whip me. Then he said he might leave me tied to a pole outside the keep for a whole week so all could see his failure. He said I'd shamed the family name, and he didn't even want to look at me. This was after several minutes of asking me why I would do it. Did I have no sense? What was I thinking?" She blew her nose on the linen square. "I feared he'd be angry enough to do them all to me. Whip me, tie me to a post, *and* send me to an island. You don't know my sire. He never makes empty threats."

"You've seen him this angry before?"

The twiddling of her thumbs started, and she didn't attempt to curb the impulse. "Not exactly. This was by far the worst thing I've ever done. The way he looked at me…'twas like he hated me. My mother said I wasn't the first soiled maiden, and my sire said I was the first of *his* to be soiled." She stopped to hitch a few times before she continued. "He said I was ruined, that I was worthless to him now, that I was the prettiest of his daughters—" the next words came out in a loud wail, "—but no one would ever want me now because I was foolish and soiled and I'd never marry and I might as well be a spinster on an island."

The abbess reached across the table and took one hand in hers. "Child, adults say many things they don't often mean when they are upset."

"Not my papa. He means everything he says," she insisted. "But all those threats did not upset me nearly as much as the last one he made."

The abbess said, "All those threats would have frightened me, although I do believe he was simply saying those things to calm his temper. Some men let their anger out in strange ways. Even so, I'm pleased he didn't turn violent. What could he say or do that would be worse?"

Constance sniffled again, then whispered, "He said he would send my younger sister Denise to a convent so she wouldn't be influenced by my mistakes. I couldn't let him hurt my sister. 'Twas not her fault."

The abbess patted her hand. "So you ran away."

"Aye, to protect my sister and because I don't want to go to the island. He owns a small island that isn't inhabited by anyone. He took us out there a few times when we were younger, just to pick shells. That place frightened me. I could not have lived out there all on my own. There wasn't even a building there, just a cave. I overheard him tell our steward to make sure the boat would be ready by the next day. So I ran away that night."

The mother abbess leaned forward and tugged Constance toward her. "I'm sure he only did it taunt you, but I thank you for telling me the truth. Is there anything else I should know?"

"Nay, 'tis everything. I'm sorry I've been such a burden, but I would like to work with the bairns, do something good for our Lord. Please do not force me to return to him." Perhaps she wouldn't have to run away after all. If the abbess accepted her and didn't force her back home, if no one else came after her, could she make a life here? She'd like to try, if only for Kelby's sake.

"How many summers are you, lass?"

"I was born in the middle of a verra cold winter. Ten and nine years ago."

She patted Constance's hand. "Then you are old enough to make your own decisions. I'll not force you to return to your sire. I'd be pleased to have your assistance with the bairns again. Wee Kelby misses you."

Constance was so excited she bounded out of her chair and wrapped her arms around the mother abbess. "My thanks to you, Mother Abbess. I vow to do as I should. I'll not stray again."

"Child," she said, reaching to unclasp Constance's hands behind her head. "You're choking me. Please release my neck."

Constance jumped back, apologizing and grinning. She'd finally told the truth, and she hadn't been punished for it. She could start over. She breathed a sigh of relief and plunked back down in the chair.

"There is only one small problem."

Constance squelched the groan that threatened to come out of her mouth. Sitting forward in her chair, she asked, "What is it?"

"I do not think those men belonged to a baron. They were dirty, disrespectful, and one of them hit me. Do those sound like your sire's men?"

"Nay. I'm so sorry they hurt you, but I don't believe my sire's guards would ever strike a woman, especially not one in an abbey. Who could they be?"

Mayhap she was wanted for the Channel of Dubh.

CHAPTER THIRTEEN

D ANIEL LED THE WAY TO the side entrance, grabbing the door handle and opening it with his new
appendage, only to find it tugged back. He clutched
his new hand, something he found himself doing often
because he was afraid he'd lose it, but it was still attached.

"What the hell?" he whispered to the others.

"Knock," said Connor.

Daniel knocked, and the door opened with a force that
would have felled him if he hadn't been quick enough to
jump out of the way. A massive brute stood there staring at
him, not speaking. Daniel hadn't dared take a good look at
the guard before, but now he stole a quick glance to take
the man's measure. He had a long scar across his face from
his left eye to his right jaw. It would be a mistake to upset
this lout.

Daniel silently held out the stone the serving lass had
given to Connor.

The brute accepted the stone, stood back, and allowed
them to pass.

Once inside, Daniel waited for his eyes to adjust, surprised to find himself in a chamber that was nearly empty
but for a serving bar with one man behind it. It had been
full before.

"Grab an ale and head that way," the barkeep said, pointing to the long passageway at the end of the chamber. "The
fighting is about to commence. What will you wager?"

"Who's fighting?" Connor asked, approaching the bar with a coin in his hand.

"Deathstalker against Ivan."

Connor said, "I'll take Deathstalker."

The others followed suit. Each of them was given an ale and a stone to vouch for his wager, then they headed down the passageway. Gregor started to ask a question, but Daniel elbowed him. "Hush until we get in there."

The din grew louder as they progressed down the dark passageway lit with small torches. When they reached the huge chamber halfway down the path, they were surprised to find probably fifty men gathered in the chamber, many seated on stools while the others paced. The dirt of the floor had been built up in a graduated manner so those in the back could see above those in the front. Benches and stools were arranged in the middle, but the rest of the chamber was standing only. Three men stood in an open area down below. Spectators could only watch from three sides. The back held stools for the contenders.

"Deathstalker must be the big one," Daniel said.

Gavin said, "What made you say that? The eyes that could pierce your soul as well as any could or is it the drool rolling down his chin?"

Gregor choked on his ale.

Daniel glared at Gavin and said, "Do either of the other two look like a death stalker?"

Connor, a wry grin crossing his face, said, "I'm not sure if he looks like a death stalker, but the man standing across from him, who can only be Ivan, looks like he's taken one too many blows to the head."

"Shut up. They're staring at us." Gregor spun around and headed toward a stool toward the back of the spectators. "What the hell are we looking for anyway?"

They each found a stool in the back row. As soon as they took their seats, the man who stood between Ivan and Deathstalker spoke to both fighters, then clasped their shoulders, stepped back, and waved his hand in a circle above his head.

The battle commenced.

Ivan dove at his competitor, knocking him down and pummeling his belly. Deathstalker gave him a fist to his jaw, sending Ivan to the ground and giving himself time to get back up, ready to fight. Once Ivan rejoined the fight, they battled for maybe two or three minutes more before Deathstalker took a swing at the other man, connected square with his temple, and knocked Ivan out completely.

The crowd shouted and applauded, many of them jumping up in the air before they sat down.

The judge stood next to Deathstalker and announced, "Deathstalker wins."

Another man appeared out of a doorway on the other end of the chamber, handing out coin to anyone who could display their winning stone.

Gavin's eyes widened when he saw the coin he was given. "That was easy. I'm wagering again."

Once they finished collecting their coin, the man in the center said, "Who's next?"

The four sat in the corner for two more rounds, watching Deathstalker take on various other competitors, before Daniel announced, "I'm going to take him on. I can beat him."

"Daniel," Connor countered, "in case you've forgotten, you only have one hand."

"I'll be using my new assistant, *Treun*."

"They won't allow you to wear it."

"We'll see."

As soon as they asked who was next, Daniel bolted out of his seat. "I am," he shouted.

"What's your name?"

Daniel glanced at his friends before he shouted back, "Damien." He wasn't about to use his real name.

"Damien the Demon? Come forward."

That wasn't exactly the moniker he would have chosen, but he wasn't about to argue. He'd done everything he could to build up his biceps at the Drummond lists, and the time had come to prove himself in front of a larger audience. With *Treun* on his arm, he had no doubt he'd be able to take on the well-named Deathstalker. As he stepped down toward the center of the platform, he heard the whispers build.

"What the hell is that?" Deathstalker asked, pointing to his fake hand.

Daniel slipped it off and handed it to the man he guessed was the judge. "I only have one hand, which would give him a distinct advantage over me. This evens us out, makes it fair."

The judge handled the fake hand, inspected it carefully before he declared. "You may don it. Place your bets. Damien or Deathstalker."

Daniel stood in one place, shaking his arms to relax his muscles as his cousins ran out to place their bets. Connor returned first and leaned over to whisper to him. "They're all betting against you. If you win, we'll make a ton of coin."

"You all bet on me, did you not?" Daniel asked.

"Och, aye!" Gavin shouted, as he entered the chamber from the passageway. "I saw you fight Cailean, the Invincible Crazed Brute, I've no doubt you'll win."

Gregor laughed and said, "Cailean would do well here."

His cousins moved closer to the fight to get a better view. A few moments after they were seated, the man swung his arm overhead and the fight began. Daniel had watched Deathstalker's moves for three fights now, and he knew he'd try the same ones against him. True, the man was huge, but he wasn't quick, which Daniel would use to his advantage.

Deathstalker made the first move by diving toward him, his arms held wide to sweep around Daniel's waist, but

Daniel side-stepped him with a shove, sending him face down into the dirt floor. The crowd bellowed their surprise at Daniel's speed.

He allowed Deathstalker to get to his feet and managed to clobber him with two hits in a row to his face—one to his jaw and the other to his temple. He saw the man's eyes react to the second blow, rolling a bit before he managed to refocus and make another swing.

Daniel dodged the blow, then swung both his false hand and his real hand back and forth in front of the brute until he was so confused, he didn't know which one was swinging toward him. He danced a full circle around Deathstalker, who spun and spun, unable to keep up with Daniel's quick moves and his confusing hands. He finally dealt the fool a hard blow to the head, and Deathstalker crumpled to his feet.

The crowd cheered Daniel on. "Damien! Damien! Damien!"

"Well done," Connor came over to him, clasped his shoulder, and handed him an ale to take a few swigs before the next fight was announced.

"Go again, Damien?"

Daniel glanced at Connor, shrugged his shoulders, and nodded.

He took on two more contenders.

By the end of the night, he'd beat four contenders and gained a new name.

He was now Damien with the Devil's Hand.

They had their in with the underground.

———

CONSTANCE ATE AS MUCH AS she could at the next meal. Ada sat with her.

"We're so glad you're out of the cellar, Constance. 'Twas not right for you to be in there. I cannot believe the mother abbess left you down there for so long." She dipped her chunk of bread into the fish stew and chewed quietly.

Constance noticed Ada giving her an odd look. Finally, she asked, "What is it, Ada?"

"I just wondered if 'tis true or not." She stared at her meal while she asked the question, for some reason not lifting her gaze to meet Constance's.

"If what is true?"

"Are you of noble blood? 'Tis the latest rumor." Ada clasped her hands in her lap and gazed at Constance. "And if so, why did you not tell me? I came to see you in the cellar. I wish to be your friend."

"Oh, Ada. Forgive me for not confiding in you. I didn't confide in anyone for the longest time. I had to tell the truth in the end. Mother Abbess gave me no choice."

Ada just nodded, staring at her hands. "I wish I were of noble blood. Then mayhap I could go home. Your home must be nicer than this."

Constance sighed. "My keep is nicer than this, true, but I can never go home. 'Tis out of the question. I would much rather spend my time caring for the bairns of the world, mostly the lost ones. You do a good job with them, Ada. Why not enjoy them?"

Ada stared at the rafters for a moment, and Constance thought she noticed tears in her eyes. "I suppose I will," Ada said at last, lowering her chin. "You make a good point. I'm sorry you had to reveal something you didn't wish to tell. Will you tell me the rest of your tale now?"

"Nay. I prefer to keep my true identity a secret. 'Tis safer that way." Though her sire had always provided for them, she knew him to be a stubborn, unforgiving man. He would undoubtedly see fit to punish anyone who helped her elude him.

"I understand. 'Twas a nasty thing the mother abbess did to you, putting you down there alone."

"No matter. 'Tis over now and I'm off to work with the wee ones again. I shall see you in the nursery." She finished her food and left in haste, wishing to end her conversation with Ada before it took a different turn.

The sweetest sight she'd ever seen greeted her in the nursery. Kelby hopped off her stool and ran toward Constance, followed by two other wee lasses. As soon as the wee bairn with the short leg reached her, she hugged her skirts, then reached her arms straight up toward her. "Constie, up?"

Constance leaned down and picked up the lassie, giving her a swift hug and a kiss on the cheek.

"More kisses?" The wee one tipped her cheek toward Constance, waiting for more.

Constance chuckled and gave her three more kisses, then settled on a stool so she could hug the other two lasses, giving each a kiss on the forehead.

Kelby looked at Constance and asked, "Find my mama?"

Constance shook her head. "Nay, lass. I'm afraid your mama is gone."

Kelby stuck her thumb in her mouth and rested her head on Constance's shoulder.

Sister Murreall made her way over to Constance. "You were missed, lass, especially by wee Kelby. I'm glad to have you back. We have a new set of wooden blocks for the wee ones to use. Why don't you sit with the lassies and show them how to stack them?"

Constance sat in the middle of a big fur and the bairns clustered around her. They stacked the blocks, making different things until they fell over and the girls all giggled. Then she told them two tales of angels and heaven, hoping to give Kelby some hope. She probably was too young to understand, but mayhap the memory would stay with her.

The bairns were totally enraptured by her voice, some of them even lying on their sides and closing their eyes for a nap. When Kelby finally fell asleep, Constance lay her down on a different fur and covered her with a plaid.

"Well done, lass," Sister Murreall said. "They need a wee

nap. They have not been sleeping well, some of them."

Constance nodded to the nun and said, "I'm going to take care of my needs. I'll be right back."

"Of course, lass."

Constance moved out into the passageway, taking her time and thanking God for sending the lassies here to give her a purpose. She hadn't gone far when the sound of horses outside carried to her.

She froze, fear pooling in her gut, then searched for a hiding place. The only one she could find was the garderobe, so she ducked inside, pulled the curtain shut, and listened.

A fist pounded on the door and one of the guards answered, "Here now, you need not beat the door down. Where are your manners?"

The man outside said, "We were approved at the gate. We should be allowed to wander through your building."

"What is your purpose?" This voice was unmistakably that of the mother abbess.

"We're looking for someone, by the request of Baron Walter Lockhart of Lee. We're to search the premises."

Constance recognized the voice as the head of her sire's guards. He did not give up easily. She closed her eyes and prayed he would go away without searching the premises. Her legs trembled so fiercely that she nearly lost her footing and fell to the ground.

"In the name of our Lord," Mother Abbess called out. "You need not be belligerent. Please remember that we are the House of our Lord and we don't submit to searches. What exactly are you looking for?"

The guard's voice carried to her easily. "We're looking for his daughter. She either ran away or was kidnapped and he wants her back. Now."

Leave it to her sire to be so demanding. His men were not as rude as the ones who had come before, but they were no less officious. They'd barged right in and started barking their demands.

The abbess continued in her calming voice. "We have no one of that name. What does she look like?"

"She has flame-red hair, long and wavy, and green eyes. She's about this tall." She could not see the gesture, but she could imagine him lifting his hand to his chest. "She would have arrived about a moon ago."

"Why are you just searching now?"

"Because we've searched all of Scotland, both the Lowlands and Highlands. And we'll not stop until we find her."

Even if they went away without finding her, everyone at the abbey would know they had come searching for her. She could no longer lie about her heritage. She could no longer hide.

The abbess said, "We have no one here who fits that description, and you'll not search our abbey. We have mass at present. Guards!" she called out through the door, "take them away."

"We'll take our leave," the guard said, his tone brusque. "If you see a lass who fits that description, you'll notify the Sheriff of Lanarkshire?"

"Of course."

The door closed and Constance nearly fell to her knees in relief, but not for long. She could not ask the abbess to continue lying for her. Her secret was out, so she had no choice.

She'd be leaving in the middle of the night.

CHAPTER FOURTEEN

———✦———

TWO DAYS LATER, THE GROUP of cousins sat at a table in the inn they were staying at in Edinburgh, eating the midday meal.

"Daniel, we've been at this a few days and learned naught. I think we should take our leave. 'Tis an empty lead."

"Nay, I don't think so," Daniel said, taking a bit of stew and chewing on the left side of his mouth. "I've heard talk of the man who's in charge. We need to find out if it's someone associated with the channel." He brought his hand up to the right side of his jaw and rubbed it. He'd taken a good punch on that side last night, and he was still annoyed he'd allowed the arse to get the blow in.

"I'm going for a shave today," Connor said. "You need one, too." He pointed at Daniel. "You're starting to look like a ruffian."

Gavin guffawed. "Your mother would kick your arse if she saw you. You've got more bruises than my arse after my sire tosses me across the lists for being lazy."

Gregor snorted, stew flying out of his mouth.

"I like my hair long," Daniel said with a shrug. "I think the beard will add to my presence. Make me look like someone who really has the devil's hand."

Gregor said, "I don't think I'd tell your mother and father the name you're using, either."

Daniel snorted. "'Tis for a good cause, and you know it."

Connor put his utensil down to stare at him. "'Tis the

truth you speak? Because I'm not so certain anymore. I think you like your new title. Are you going to be able to walk away at the end of this?"

The words bit into Daniel, for they were more than a little true. He had to admit he felt a bit heady from the attention he was getting for being so fierce and powerful, something he'd never experienced before. He liked hearing the crowd call his name—well, not his name precisely, but Damien's name. It made him feel...important. Seen. But he didn't want the others to know that. Looking at his food, he said, "Of course I can walk away, but not until I've learned something. I'm telling you I've almost found out who the leader is. There could be a relationship between this group and the Channel of Dubh. I'm going to ask tonight if there's a way I can make more coin."

Gavin dropped his tone for effect. "You cannot bear to leave. Why not? You are being quite mysterious, Daniel Damien Demon Devil's Hand, or whatever your name is. You'll not get away with keeping secrets from us."

Daniel gnawed off another chunk of bread to keep his hand busy.

"I know why this is important to him—and she has red hair," Gregor said.

Gregor was always a wee bit more intuitive than the others. But right now, Daniel didn't feel inclined to thank him for it. He spun around to glare at Gregor on the bench next to him. "What the hell does Constance have to do with this? Naught. Is it so odd that I like a wee bit of attention? That I appreciate being seen as strong instead of crippled? Connor, everyone looks at you and sees Alexander Grant reborn. Gavin, you're the great Logan Ramsay's only son, and your mother is the best archer in all the land. And Gregor, your mother is the most renowned healer in the land and you're her only son and the son of a famous laird. What the hell am I? A second son who's naught but a cripple. When people look at me, they see only what I lack. They pity me. Is it any surprise I like this attention and why they wager on me?"

Connor gave him a look that said he wasn't having any of it. "You're the lad who gained a reputation for being able to slip in and out of situations without being seen. You do it so well that you've earned the nickname 'Ghost.' Is that not enough for you? Besides, if 'Damien' becomes any more infamous, you'll never be able to slip in and out of places unseen. Your fame will kill your ghost."

Daniel stood from the table. "Nay, 'tis not enough. And it wasn't enough for Constance either. She ran back to the abbey because she thinks I won't be able to protect her. And until Jennet gave me this hand, I didn't believe in myself either." He was so upset, he stormed out of the room, nearly knocking the bench over, and ran out into the gray, foggy day.

Hellfire, but he hadn't planned on revealing that last part. He also hated to admit that Connor was probably correct. He wouldn't be able to move about freely in Edinburgh anymore. People would remember him.

He raced across the main road, wandered aimlessly, and then found a huge tree to lean against. He'd needed to leave the room at once, or he would have started throwing things. His cousins didn't understand.

He didn't wish to feel sorry for himself, but now that he'd felt the power, he couldn't bring himself to relinquish it. Not yet.

He hadn't been there long when Connor approached him. He stopped just opposite him. "You're right about one thing. Losing your hand was far more difficult to overcome than anything I've had to do. But you have one talent that puts you way above the rest of us."

"What the hell are you talking about?" Daniel said, his arms crossed.

"You have the quickest mind of any of us. Anyone can learn to swing a sword or shoot a bow, but no one can learn how to be clever. 'Tis a gift you've been given. Don't lose it over something as inconsequential as fighting for wagers. Be powerful and wise for a purpose, not just to gain a name for yourself. A name in the underground is worthless, and 'tis not a reputation to be proud of." He paused, then added, "And I don't think you're seeing the situation with Constance clearly. You're besotted and it's clouding your judgment."

"What? I have no idea what you are talking about. I thought we had a chance, and she ran away. What else is there to know?"

Gavin and Gregor came up behind Connor.

"What else?" Connor continued. "Have you considered why she chose to stay at the abbey rather than travel with her friend? Why she stopped talking to anyone after those men approached Braden's gate? That poor lass is clearly running from something or someone. She's fighting to survive, and that battle took precedence over her relation-ship with you. You let her go because you believed she thought you less of a man. You were wrong, Daniel, and you'll regret it someday if you don't help her."

"I agree with Connor," Gavin said, uncharacteristically serious. "Don't take yourself out of Constance's life yet. As far as the underground goes—if you wish to go back one more night, we'll support you, but we need to return to our team on the morrow."

Gregor said, "Aye, for all we know, something else may have come up and we're searching the wrong city."

"I hope you'll come with us," Connor said. He clasped Daniel's shoulder and said, "Too many blows to your head, and you'll not be thinking like Ghost any longer but more like Ivan."

Daniel couldn't help but laugh at that.

"I'm going back in to finish eating," Connor said. "Please join us when you're ready."

The three returned to the inn while he continued to

lean against the tree. They'd given him something to think about. Had he been wrong about sweet Constance?

Possibly, but could he walk away when he was winning? He doubted it. He liked his title—Damien with the Devil's Hand. Or just Devil's Hand.

No shave, no fussing with his hair.

And his *two* hands.

———◆———

CONSTANCE SWIPED HER HANDS ACROSS the trews she'd donned under her gown one more time. She'd thought of just wearing the trews but decided the layers would keep her warmer. She stayed hidden in her chamber, waiting until the middle of the night to make her escape. Ada had agreed to meet her out in the gardens at midnight to help her get over the fence.

She just had to get away.

All this turmoil had proven too much for her. Every night her stomach had been upset, ever since the first set of men had arrived at the abbey in search of a flame-haired lass. She still had no idea why that first group was after her, though she knew her father wanted to find her for one reason: so he could punish her.

She pulled the red stone from her pocket and was rubbing it for luck one last time when something occurred to her.

Daniel had mentioned the stone might be valuable. What if he was right? Mayhap she could use it to barter a ride on a cart to Grant land. She'd hate to give it up because it belonged to her dear mother, but she would do whatever she had to in order to stay alive.

Then another thought occurred to her, something she'd never considered. What if this stone was extremely valuable and her mother had reported it missing to her sire? Could it be possible that he sought her out because she'd stolen the gemstone? Or mayhap they would find it and track her whereabouts?

Her eyes widened, and she shoved the necklace back into her pocket, vowing to keep it hidden.

When the time came, she crept down the staircase and out the side door. No one was about so she crept out to the bench to wait for Ada, but to her surprise, the lass was already there.

Ada held something out to her. "Here. I brought this for you. 'Tis a dagger and you may need it."

Constance stared at it, her eyes tearing up at the thought that she might indeed need it.

"Are you sure you wish to go to Grant land, Constance? Why not go to the castle where Rose's friend lives? You've been there before. Do you not believe they would help you? They would be better suited to guide you to Grant land."

She'd considered that possibility, but Daniel wouldn't be there any longer. Still, Ada was right—they had been kind to her there. Perhaps they would send someone to travel with her.

"I don't think 'twould be safe to go to the Grant land on your own," Ada continued. "'Tis too far away from what you tell me. I asked Mother Abbess about Clan Grant and she told me they are far, far away. I don't wish to see you hurt."

Constance shook her head. She didn't know what to believe or where to go. All she wished she could do was find Daniel. Or Rose. She fought to keep her tears of self-pity inside, knowing that once the dam broke she'd be deluged.

Ada said, "Go to Muir Castle. I think you'll be safer there. 'Tis only a short jaunt compared to the other journey, and you'll have a better chance of success. The wild animals, the reivers…how would you fight them off alone?"

Constance thought for a moment and said, "Mayhap you're right. I think I could find my way there though 'twill take me half a day to walk."

"You should be there before dawn if you don't stop. Here." She handed over a bundle of cloth. "Here's the monk's mantle for you to wear, as we discussed. Any reivers should leave you alone if they think you're a man of the cloth."

"How I wish I could steal a horse, but I don't dare attempt it."

"Aye, you're not a thief either," Ada said.

She wished that were true, but hadn't she stolen her mother's gemstone? There was no denying it, even though she hadn't considered it stealing at the time. She couldn't regret it. The stone had given her comfort and strength, almost as if her mother were with her.

"Are you sure you wish to go?" Ada reached for her hand.

"Aye." The gesture reminded her of Rose. Oh, how she missed her dear friend, but she had to forge ahead on her own. If she left now, she could be at Grant land before winter arrived.

"Do you wish for me to go along with you?"

Ada's question pulled her out of her melancholy. "Nay," she shouted, dropping Ada's hand and clapping her hand over her mouth to mask the loud sound. She would not have anyone else hurt because of her. "'Tis not safe. I remember the way to Muir Castle. I think you're right. I'll start there, and if they'll not help me, I'll make my way to Grant Castle on my own."

"I think 'tis a wise decision," Ada whispered. "I have something else for you." Ada handed her another wrapped package. "There's a hunk of cheese and bread inside. I took it while I worked in the kitchens yester eve. Use your dagger if you must. Keep it hidden in the pocket of the monk's garment. And keep your hood up so they'll not notice your red hair."

She gave Ada a big hug. "My thanks to you. You've been

verra kind to me."

"Godspeed, lass. I hope you find him."

"Him?"

Her friend smiled at her knowingly. "I know who your heart pines for. Go and find him. He'll protect you."

"Oh, Ada. If I could just find Rose, I'd be ecstatic. Daniel and me? I don't think so. He's of noble blood, and me?"

Ada cast her a sideways glance. "I think you're the baron's daughter, are you not? The one those men came searching for earlier?"

She sighed, resigned to tell all at this point. The battle to protect her identity was now over. "Aye, 'tis me. But I've shamed my clan."

Ada gasped, apparently understanding exactly what would bring shame to her clan, but then she hugged Constance. "You're a kind-hearted lass. You'll find your way somehow. Now go. You need to get there before the sun comes up."

Ada helped her over the fence, then waved goodbye.

Constance's heart raced as she crept down the length of the hedges toward the front of the abbey. Following the curtain wall, she peeked around the corner, pleased to see the guard at the main entrance asleep with his back against the wall. Most of the time, very little happened at the front gate.

She soon found the main path they had followed to Muir Castle. It would probably take her several hours to walk there, mayhap the entire day if she had to keep hiding.

She set off at a brisk pace, keeping her ears alert to all sounds around her. Her first two hours were uneventful. She noticed familiar trees along the way, valleys and burns that told her she was traveling the same way she'd traveled with Daniel. Thank goodness it was a cloudless night so the moon could help her find her way. The journey would have been quite enjoyable if it hadn't been for her belly churning over every little sound.

In fact, she could swear there was an owl that appeared to be following her, its soft hoot always a bit over her right shoulder.

Guessing she was halfway there, she gauged that if the journey continued to go well, she might arrive before dawn, which would please her immensely. She was just rounding a bend when she caught something out of the corner of her eye.

Unfortunately, that person caught sight of her, as well.

She had her hood up so there was no remark about her red hair, but she didn't wish to be seen up close. Racing off in the opposite direction, she eventually found a path that a horse would never be able to pass through.

The voices behind her drew closer. "Leave him be," one of them said. "'Twas just a monk."

"Mayhap he's got some coin to share with us, but you need not share if you've no interest. I'll keep it to myself, arsehole."

She continued on the narrow path, hoping she could slip into a copse of trees ahead where she could hide, but they caught up to her.

"He's headed down a footpath. You cannot go that way. Leave him be. The Lord will make us pay if you hurt a monk."

Then the worst thing imaginable happened. A branch caught her hood, tugging it down to her shoulders. She prayed they'd already turned around.

They had not.

"'Tis the red-haired lass in disguise!" one shouted.

"Get her!"

Constance screamed and ran as hard as she could.

CHAPTER FIFTEEN

D ANIEL APPROACHED THE SIDE ENTRANCE of
The Hound and the Stag alone. His cousins planned
on waiting in the tavern before following him. He moved
down the stairs quickly, not speaking to anyone, and
knocked on the door at the base of the stairs.

The scarred doorman, whom he'd taken to calling Scarface, though he was not foolish enough to do so to the
fellow's face, opened the door and said to him, "He got
you good last night. 'Tis quite a black eye you've got, lad."
He chuckled but didn't follow him.

When he reached the man who handled the wagers in
the first chamber, he decided it was time to start asking
questions.

The man greeted him with a smile. "Damien. Glad
you're back. You've made us some good coin over the last
few days. Here's your cut of that."

Daniel pocketed it. "My thanks, but I need more. What
else can I do to earn more coin?"

"Ah, an enterprising lad, are you? Perhaps we can be of
service. Wait here."

With that, he disappeared down the passageway. He
returned a moment later with the judge who decided the
fights. The judge beckoned wordlessly for him to follow,
and the man with the coin winked at him before slipping
back behind the bar.

Together, Daniel and the judge walked down the pas-

sageway to the fighting chamber. The space felt so large
and hollow when it was empty.

"You want more coin?" the man finally asked. "I may
have an opportunity for you, but you'd have to be willing
to leave Edinburgh."

"I can move around. I need not stay here."

The judge gave him a long, appraising look, then said,
"There is a way, but you'll have to win two more fights for
us in the large chamber."

Daniel had no idea what he was referring to. "The large
chamber?"

He tipped his head toward the back of the room, where
the passageway continued. "The back chamber is much
larger. Anything is allowed. Only our best fighters are
given the chance. Betting is wild because there tends to
be more blood. In the front chamber, gentleman's rules
are used. No kicking in the bollocks. In the back chamber,
you'll get kicked every which way, but you'll make good
coin. If you survive those two fights, we'll send you on
another quest. One that could bring you more coin than
you could ever imagine."

"What quest?" Daniel couldn't contain his excitement.
He was finally getting closer to the Channel of Dubh. He
was sure of it.

"You can join our men in the channel."

"What is the channel?" he asked, somehow managing to
sound casual.

"The men work about once a moon. They're sent to
pick up cargo, mostly in the north, but it needs to be taken
east. Come this way. I'll let you talk to the head of this
venture."

He led Daniel through the front fighting chamber, guiding him toward a much larger chamber nearly at the end
of the passageway. "This is where you'll fight. As you can
see, we can hold many more spectators back here. The
wagers are much higher."

Daniel glanced around, noticing it was double the size of the front chamber. The floor had dark stains in spots. Blood.

The judge must have noticed his stares because he added, "Aye, men have died back here. Anything goes with the fists."

Daniel said, "I can handle myself." He lifted his chin in the hopes of giving the impression of confidence. Now all he had to do was convince himself. In the end, the danger didn't matter—if this was the only way he'd get access to the channel, he had to do it. He had to survive.

The judge nodded and spun on his heel, leading him to a small door at the very end of the passageway. Someone inside grunted in response to his knock, and he opened the door and gestured for Daniel to follow him. The small chamber was full of tables stacked with coin. The space was empty but for one man surrounded by four guards. The man's back was to them as they entered the chamber.

"Damien here wants to earn more coin. He wants into the channel."

The man spun around and Daniel nearly choked. Blair Lamont stood in front of him. He'd grown his hair longer, but there was no mistaking him. Blair and his brother had killed Cairstine's clan and stolen her castle—and the brother had claimed her as his wife, although no vows had ever been exchanged. The black-hearted bastard who'd fathered Steenie was now dead, but his brother had survived and escaped. They'd suspected he would return to the Channel of Dubh, and so he had. Daniel was on the cusp of learning very important information. He could not risk any mistakes.

Lamont stared at him, and for a moment, Daniel feared he would recognize him, but then he realized that was foolish. Why would Blair remember him? The man had moved away from Drummond land years ago, when Daniel was but a child. He might remember his parents, but he wouldn't remember him.

"He has to prove himself to get into the channel." Blair dropped his gaze back to his task, sorting coins into bags.

"I'll do whatever it takes," Daniel said at once. "I want coin."

"Why?"

Daniel thought quickly. "Because I wish to travel east. I want to go to France."

"You have two tasks to complete before you can work in the channel. The first is to win two fights in the large chamber. And you'll be up against some powerful men. They'll not be easy fights."

"No problem. I can do that."

"Once you do, I'll send you on another verra lucrative mission. The first two groups I sent failed to do the job. If you fail me too, I may have to cut your throat."

Daniel said, "I'll not fail you. What is it?"

"Find the red-haired lass with the red gemstone. I'll tell you where she is once you've finished your fights."

Daniel nearly choked.

CONSTANCE RAN AS HARD AS she could, but to no avail. She screamed when one of the men grabbed her hood and yanked her backward. She landed on her back, the wind knocked out of her.

Two faces loomed over her, only to be attacked by an owl.

"What the hell? Get that bird away from me!" The bird swooped down three times before one of the men caught it with the flat of his sword, sending it fluttering away.

"Do ye think she's the one they want?"

"Aye, she has to be. We'll get her to Lamont and collect our coin."

"Or we market her to the highest bidder. I heard she's of a noble blood and her sire's guards are searching for her.

Mayhap the nobleman would pay more than Lamont."

"Nay, we take her to Lamont. There's another group of bastards looking for her, too. I know not who they work for, but they'll skin us alive just for their fun before they take her. Nay, we'll go to Lamont."

Constance coughed when her breath finally returned. "Please, I'm sure the Grants will pay you coin if you take me to them." She pushed herself to a sitting position, eyeing her assailants. There was no point in fighting until she knew what she was up against.

Know thine enemy.

That had been one of the morals of the stories her sire used to tell them, stories of the fae that ran in the forests and other mystical creatures.

Papa, forgive me.

What else had her sire told them? She could remember her brothers asking him questions about war.

He'd said the best weapon a person had was his mind.

She'd do him proud and pay attention. Up until her transgression, her sire had always treated her with approval and even affection. A sharp feeling of longing pulled at her, but he would never accept her as his daughter again. Her sire was a fierce warrior, and everyone in the family knew not to trifle with him when he had his "warrior look" on.

He'd given her that warrior look in his solar as he threatened punishment after punishment.

But the hot shame she felt whenever she remembered his censure would not help her escape this situation. Her mind was the only thing that could do that. She may not be able to outrun these fools, but she could outthink them, could she not? Daniel would believe in her, and she knew Rose would, too. Wiping the dirt from her hands, she rose to her feet and took two steps back until she leaned against a tree, hoping it would support her trembling legs.

One man was much larger than the other, but the small one kept barking orders at him. They both wore old plaids, their pattern now unrecognizable because of wear and dirt. The men's unkempt appearance suggested they were reivers who lived the land, robbing from others. Each horse had two heavy saddlebags, probably full of stolen items they would sell later. Their faces looked as though they hadn't see a wet linen square in years, dirt etched deep into wrinkles from the sun.

"Grants? Hellfire, I'm not going near them. They'll cut me to pieces and feed me to the vultures first. I don't bother with the Grants."

"I say we take her to her sire's guards," the big man suggested.

The smaller one shook his head in apparent annoyance. "I told you. She goes to Lamont. He's the easiest and we'll get paid well. No risk involved. We'll have her there in two days. Now get over here, missy, and get on that horse." He pointed to the closer beast.

"Let her ride with me," the other one said, his eyes pointing in two different directions. One eye glanced up and down before he reached for her. "What kind of titties have you under that monk's outfit?"

Fear trailed a path up Constance's spine, but the big man's friend slapped his hand away. "Nay, do not touch her. She's of noble blood."

"Not no more. Now she's a peasant just like the rest of us, and I want to bed her before we take her back. Please, Malcolm?"

"I said nay. She rides with me. And when we get there, she'll not be telling Lamont we touched her or he'll cut off your shaft and mine, too."

"Hellfire, Malcolm. You never let me have any fun." He wiped the snot running from his nose with his sleeve. "I like her. She's pretty."

"If we get her to Lamont in two days, I'll give you enough coin for a whore in Edinburgh."

His face lit up. "All right. I can wait. Then I can do anything I want."

Constance hoped she'd gained a friend in Malcolm, but his expression didn't look promising. His beady eyes seemed to be constantly assessing her.

At least he didn't intend to force himself on her. And at least there were only two of them. If luck was on her side, she'd be able to escape.

The beady-eyed one lifted her up onto his horse, letting his hand linger on her backside. She swung at him, but he climbed up behind her in one swift movement and easily stilled her fist. "Touching never hurt nobody," he said with a sneer. Then he chuckled and squeezed one of her breasts.

"Malcolm, why do you get to touch her if I can't?" his partner shouted at him.

"Never mind. There's no' much there, so dinnae worry yourself. I'll stop."

"But can I not sleep next to her when we stop?" The big one gave her an odd smile that looked more like a sneer, his two missing teeth quite obvious.

"Nay. She stays with me so you don't ruin this for us. This could be the most coin we've ever earned. 'Tis as I said. I'll find you another in Edinburgh."

Constance wanted to gag.

How would she get away from these two louts?

She didn't know how, but she vowed she would.

———————

DANIEL TOOK ANOTHER FIST TO the face, groaned and fell back onto the ground. The judge stepped in and said, "Pause for a drink."

The patrons were rowdier in the back chamber, and they did their share of shouting and hollering at the two combatants. All Daniel could do was force himself up and into the corner, where his stool was perched next to a bucket of water. He wiped the blood from his mouth with the linen lying across the stool.

The announcer said, "Devil's Hand against Evil King will continue in five minutes. Place your bets for the second round of fighting."

Daniel took a swig of water and spat it out. A lad of about twelve summers scuttled up to him and said, "I've been assigned to help you, Devil's Hand." He used a piece of linen to wipe the blood out of Daniel's eye. "Here, we put this on to stop the bleeding." He put some concoction on the injured eye with his right hand, which was when something else caught Daniel's attention.

"Call me Damien. What happened to your left hand, lad?" Just like Daniel, he didn't have one, although his arm ended in a clean stump that lacked any scar tissue.

"I was born this way. Where'd you get your hand? Who made it? I want one."

"'Twas made by a friend. Not in Edinburgh. What's your name?"

"My name's Terric. You should put something on the end of that. Then you'd beat them all since the judge has allowed you to have it."

"What?"

Terric held up a small cup of water for Daniel. "Put a blade in it and you'll kill all of them."

"I cannot kill them. 'Tis not what the fight is about." He sighed. "I may not last through this one." He wasn't faring well, but somehow he had to stick it out. He had to be the one to find Constance. He couldn't allow anyone else to touch her. Constance was his.

"If not a blade, how about some piece like this? I have to use this sometimes when I'm sleeping on the streets." He pulled out a curved piece of metal with odd protruding shapes at the four edges. "Hits harder than a fist does. Stops them all."

"Where'd you get that?"

"My sire had it made for me before he died. He wanted me to always be able to protect myself."

"One minute left to wager!" the announcer called out.

Daniel's gaze swept the large chamber, amazed by the number of men who'd come to watch him fight. He noticed Connor toward the back, sitting quietly with his arms crossed in front of him.

"Here, try it," Terric said.

The two worked furiously to tuck it into the leather on the end of Daniel's hand. Probably not ethical, but what the hell was ethical in the underground world of gambling? He'd do whatever it took to save Constance from the channel.

Terric stepped back and said, "Get him."

Daniel made it to his feet just in time for the start of the next round of fighting. Evil King came at him and knocked him back on his arse with a stiff fist under his jaw. Daniel saw a few stars, but he wouldn't give up. He took one kick to his belly, barely dodging a blow to his groin, but that did it. If the bastard was going to fight dirty, then so would he.

Daniel roared to life from the ground and became Damien with a sudden burst of energy.

CHAPTER SIXTEEN

D ANIEL GOT UP, BENDING AT the waist to make his
opponent think he was stumbling to get up. He knew
the fool would only expect a swing from his right arm. At
the last second, he came at him with his left, taking him
completely by surprise. Daniel heard the crunch of bone in
the man's jaw. He fell backward but stayed up. The crowd
roared, screaming "Devil, Devil, Devil…" Daniel used the
lad's tool and his own fist to pummel his opponent's belly.
As soon as the other man bent at the waist, Daniel swung
his fist into a power strike under the man's chin, sending
him to the ground.

The crowd screamed when the judge called the win
in his favor. He glanced over at Terric, who grinned and
jumped up and down, clapping.

The men ran to collect their coin and the crowd thinned.
Connor joined him while Gavin and Gregor moved with
the crowd, hoping to hear something about the channel.

The judge came over and patted his shoulder. "Well
done, Damien. I thought you were done. Nice comeback."

Daniel asked, "My part?"

The man tossed him a few coins, then said, "You'll get
the rest when you talk to the man in charge on the morrow. He'd like to see you in the morn."

"Who's the lad?" Connor asked, motioning to Terric
with his chin.

Despite Connor's height, the lad seemed undaunted.

"I'm Terric. I help the fighters. They pay me in food. Keeps me from starving."

Daniel handed a coin to the lad. "Here. You've earned it."

"My thanks for your generosity," he said as he pocketed it. "Can I tend ye on the morrow? But I do need my weapon back."

"Aye." He watched Terric leave but then was bothered by something. He thought of his cousins Loki and Kenzie, who had lived on the streets before being taken into Clan Grant. It was a hard life, likely even more so for a lad with one hand.

"Where do you sleep, Terric?"

The lad turned around and said, "They allow me to sleep in the stables if I clean them out. I only have to sleep outside when 'tis really busy."

Connor glanced at Daniel, who offered, "Here's your weapon though you won't need it this night. Come to the inn with the Ram's head and I'll buy you a real bed for the night. Get yourself some food and meet me there later."

Connor waved to Terric. Excitement had eaten away at his world weariness, making him look like a bairn again. "Why are there so many lads without homes in Edinburgh?"

"'Tis unfortunate. He loaned me something I think I'll have made for myself." He explained the new weapon to Connor, who said naught until he finished.

Finally, his cousin said, "You look like hell, Damien. Let's go back to our inn."

Daniel stood and leaned toward Connor, only realizing his balance was out of alignment when he nearly fell. His cousin wrapped an arm around his shoulder to steady him and guided him out of the nearly empty establishment.

"'Tis time to stop this madness," Connor said in an undertone as they reached the street. "Do you not agree? You took a hell of a beating this time. Your face may never be the same."

Daniel whispered, "Nay. I must return." His gaze moved from one side of the building to the other, but then he said, "I'll explain, but wait until we're free of this place."

The two left and found their way to their inn, where they met up with Gavin and Gregor in the main room. Gregor stared at him and said, "God's teeth, but you look awful. What have you decided? Are you ready to give it up?"

They found a table in the corner where no one paid them any mind. Daniel whispered, "I met one of the owners. Blair Lamont." He held up his hand to keep anyone from commenting. "Keep it quiet. We know not who might be listening."

The three nodded, then leaned forward, anxious to hear more. "I have to continue. If I win one more fight, they'll let me in on the channel…"

"Shite, you finally got inside, did you not?" Gavin asked with an excited grin.

"Aye, 'tis why I cannot quit now."

Gavin hit the table with the palm of his hand. "I knew it. We are in the right place. You have to stay."

Daniel held his hand up to stop him from finishing. Though he could remind Gavin of how he'd urged them to return home just the day before, there was no point. That was Gavin. "There's more," he said instead.

Gregor screeched, "There is?"

"Keep your voice down," Connor said, listening raptly. "Go on."

"Lamont wishes to send me on a special mission to locate a red-haired lass with a red gemstone." He sat back and waited for their reaction.

"Constance? Are you sure 'tis her?" Connor asked.

"Does she have a gemstone?" Gavin placed both hands on the table and leaned toward Daniel.

"Aye, she showed it to me at Castle Muir. 'Twas her mother's. She calls it her lucky stone. Someone must have seen it, but I don't understand why Lamont's people would be searching for her in particular."

Connor pursed his lips and said, "I knew she was hiding from something. What if her sire's a noble?"

"He must be," Gavin said, "or his wife wouldn't have gems. Constance must have run away and grabbed the gemstone before she left."

Gregor added, "And her sire is searching for her. But why would she run away?"

Connor scratched his head. "There's still something missing here. The men who came looking for a lass at Braden's did not look like nobleman's guards…and I doubt Constance's sire hired Lamont."

"Aye," said Daniel. "Those reivers asked if we had any lasses we didn't want. I suspect they were collecting lasses for the channel. I know not if they had any knowledge about Constance at all." He paused, then added, "Something else Constance said to me makes me wonder what happened."

"What is it?" Connor asked.

"She said her sire hates her. It sounded as if she never wished to see him again."

Connor said, "Ah, that explains it."

"What? That tells me naught," Gavin said, looking exasperated.

Connor shrugged one shoulder. "'Tis about a lad. At her age, it had to be about marriage."

Daniel couldn't disagree with Connor's reasoning. "Whatever caused her to run away, I cannot leave until I find a way to help her. I have to stay and fight. Will you stay?"

Connor sighed. "I think we need some assistance. A nobleman's guards, Blair Lamont, a big gemstone. All could add up to big trouble. I'll stay with you. You two," he nodded toward Gavin and Gregor, "return and update Will and Maggie."

Daniel added, "And when you return, we may not be here. If I win, I'll be off in search of Constance if I have my way."

Finally, he felt worthy of her love. Now he could protect his bluebell.

He was a champion, if only in the underworld, and he had two hands.

———◆———

CONSTANCE FEIGNED HER OWN SLEEP, waiting for the two reivers to start snoring. They'd stolen some ale from a hut they'd passed, then drank heavily until they both passed out. She waited another fifteen minutes before she got up from her spot and crept over to one of the horses, choosing the one she'd ridden earlier.

Unfortunately, just as she was about to mount the beast, he whinnied loud enough to awaken Malcolm.

"What the hell are you doing?" His beady eyes lit with a fury she'd not often seen. She took off at a dead run, but he followed her and threw himself at her, landing on top of her with a grunt.

Constance panted, trying to catch her breath, as he forced his full weight on her. He rolled her onto her back and held her arms over her head, his face so close to hers she wished to vomit form the stench of his ale-soaked breath. "I should have kenned you'd try something. I'll be tying you up from here on. And if you try to run away again, I'll let my brother have you, but not until I taste you first. You try my patience, lassie."

He got up and yanked her to her feet, slapping her hard on her cheek. He woke his brother with a kick and made him hold on to her while he tied her hands. "We're leaving now."

He was about to toss her up on the horse when he paused for a moment. "Mayhap you need a headache. That should keep you from trying to escape."

He punched her in the jaw, snapping her head off to the side.

Constance fought tears, not wanting to give him the satisfaction. But he'd done as he'd promised.

Now she had a searing headache. When would her nightmare end?

———————

DANIEL AND CONNOR SLEPT IN one chamber while Gavin and Gregor slept across the passageway from them. Terric slept in the common room, where the innkeeper kept multiple beds for a lower price.

Daniel didn't sleep well, mostly because he hurt in so many places, but he was sound asleep when the thunderstorm came upon them.

A roar of thunder woke both of them, and Connor cursed loudly. "Hell, but I've seen enough thunderstorms for one year." He rolled over in bed and covered his head with a fur.

Daniel sat up on the edge of his bed, then moved over to the window, opening the shutters and staring out over the back of the inn. He was only there for a few moments when several brilliant flashes of lightning caused him to back away from the window. Thunder roared through their chamber and Connor finally sat up in bed. "I give up."

Daniel had turned to glance at his cousin when he heard a voice that sounded as if it were right outside the window.

"You must help her."

He spun around and stared. An apparition floating in midair outside the window stared at him. The ghost, the woman, whatever she was, wore a white gown with bell sleeves and a blue band around her waist. Her full skirts billowed beneath her as if she were buffeted by the wind of the storm. She had red hair much like Constance, curly waves bouncing in the breeze.

"You were right, Connor. I've taken too may blows to

my head." He leaned on the edge of the window, staring out over the stables behind the inn.

"What are you looking at?" Connor asked as another bolt of lightning lit up the sky.

"I'm not sure, but she looks a bit like Constance. Come look for yourself. You won't believe me otherwise." Transfixed by the floating specter in front of him, Daniel motioned to Connor without turning his head.

Connor gasped as he approached him. "Nay, nay, nay. Not this again!"

"What?" Daniel whispered. "You've seen her before?"

Connor moved closer to the window, the two of them now standing shoulder to shoulder as the ghostly apparition floated in the air directly in front of them.

"Aye," was all Connor said. "Though something is different about her." He stared at the vision, assessing her carefully.

"You must save her," the ghost said, "You are the only one who can help her." Her finger came up to point at Daniel. "Three. There are three." She then pointed to Connor, lifting her hand up to show him three fingers.

"Where are her pearls? She had pearls around her neck before."

She started to dissipate, but Daniel leaned out the window. "Who? Who are we supposed to save?"

Connor clasped Daniel's shoulder and said, "Constance. Trust me. She protects the lasses of the abbeys."

The ghost smiled and pointed at Connor, nodding her head before she disappeared with one last comment, "She needs *you*, Daniel." Then she held up a red gem shaped like a heart in her hand.

Daniel closed the shutters and latched them, plopping down on the bed. "I'd think I'd lost my mind if you hadn't seen her, too."

Connor sighed. "'Tis the second time I've seen her. She warned Roddy about Rose. Said almost the same exact thing. The only difference was she wore pearls around her neck last time. I told him never to mention it again, and I'm telling you the same thing. Do not tell Gavin or Gregor."

"And you saw the gem she held in her hand?"

"I did." Connor ran his hand across his forehead and down his face. "It only means one thing, and I think you can guess what that is."

Daniel stared up at the ceiling. "Aye, Constance is in trouble."

CHAPTER SEVENTEEN

DANIEL AND CONNOR BID FAREWELL to Gavin and Gregor after they finished breaking their fast, and their cousins rode off to Ramsay land. Then Daniel sent Terric out with several coins, charging him with getting a similar tool made for his arm attachment. There were two blacksmiths in town, and Terric knew one, so he promised to do as instructed.

When he and Connor were finally alone at the inn, he said, "I cannot take you with me, but I'd appreciate you following me." He stared at the swirling beverage in his goblet.

"I plan to. How will you approach Lamont and what exactly do you think he can do for you?"

"I asked many questions of the man in charge before the fight last eve. He said they send a few men out to the channel once every moon to pick up a shipment in the north and then bring it to the east coast. The number varies. He's been offered extra coin to find the red-haired lass. My guess is they plan to send her away too, although he didn't say so."

"Why?" Connor stroked his chin as he stared at his goblet of mead. "This is a most strange situation."

"Aye. Who would knowingly risk selling a nobleman's daughter to the channel? Even if her sire is angry with her, he's bound to retaliate."

"We're missing something."

"She's a popular lass all of a sudden, for one who was living in an abbey," Daniel declared, scratching his whiskers.

"That gemstone must be valuable," Connor said. "Even the ghost knew about it. Why did she keep saying three? What is the meaning of three? Three days? Three men have her?" He stared at Daniel. "Any ideas?"

"My guess is that we have to find her within three days. That makes the most sense as Blair said he was sending me out in two days. I fight again tonight and on the morrow I leave."

"Nay, it could take you three days to find her. We're nearly two days from the abbey."

Daniel pushed himself away from the table and stood, tossing a couple of coins on the table as payment for their food. "I'm going to meet with him right now and see what he offers me."

Connor said, "You surely grow a quick beard. Hell, but I think it's doubled in length in a sennight."

Daniel grinned. "Aye. I think the unruliness adds to my image."

They started down the main path toward The Hound and the Stag. "And what exact image are you hoping for, Damien?" Connor intentionally drawled out his false name.

"There he is! Damien with the Devil's Hand." A young lad off to the side stopped to point to him.

"Devil's Hand, are you fighting this eve? All my coin is on you," the lad's companion asked.

Daniel tipped his head to the man and said, "Aye, I'll be there this eve."

They continued on and listened to the talk in the courtyard as they passed in front of Edinburgh Castle.

"He's the toughest fighter they have. I heard he nearly killed a man last eve."

Another said, "We have to go this eve."

"He's one of fiercest fighters I've ever seen."

Daniel said with a sly grin, "All that. 'Tis exactly the image I want—tough, brutal, the best."

Connor muttered in a low voice, "Because you think 'tis what Constance wants?"

They reached their destination, but Daniel pulled Connor back from the entrance. "You wait here. And aye, I think Constance would be proud of me."

Connor chuckled and crossed his arms. "You think any lass would approve of the way you look?"

Daniel scowled. "I don't look that bad."

Connor arched his brow at him. "And you think lasses want to be afraid of their husbands?"

"Who said I wish to be her husband?"

"I did. You may be young, but 'tis exactly what you need. You're carrying on just like your sire did when he lost his heart to your mother. I've heard all the stories about Uncle Micheil. He followed her everywhere, trying to show her that other lads were poorly suited for her. He even jousted to gain her favor, show her how strong he was. Jousting, fighting. What's the difference?"

"I'm not at all like my sire. David is like my sire, not me." He spun on his heel and headed toward the side entrance, waving his hand at Connor.

"I'll return shortly." He opened the door, ready to show his special stone to Scarface. He wouldn't think about what Connor had said because it for certes held no truth.

Or did it?

It always surprised him when someone compared him to his sire. Surely his brother, who was whole and strong and steadfast, was more like Micheil Ramsay. And yet, their mother had oft told him that he reminded her of his sire as a young man, of the young warrior who'd had the strength to take down the best of the English knights in a jousting competition in Edinburgh. He'd heard Uncle Logan and Aunt Gwyneth talk about him many times.

They also talked about how Micheil had done it all to

earn the respect and catch the eye of Diana Drummond.

Was Connor right? Was he doing this to impress Constance?

He couldn't think about that now. He had to focus.

He expected the doorman to just wave him inside, but the big brute surprised him. "Enter, Damien. Nice fight last night. We've already heard we'll have to turn many away tonight. The man in charge of wagers is taking payments to reserve seats just to watch you and your Devil's Hand."

"My thanks. Where is he?"

"Head on down to the back chamber to see the owners."

He took the steps two at a time, ducking at the bottom because the door was so short. He nodded a greeting to those he saw along the way to the back chamber. To his surprise, they all treated him as if he belonged. He knocked on the door and entered when he heard Lamont's voice call out to him.

"Greetings," he said, watching the two men carefully. "Am I still on the schedule for this eve?"

Blair turned around with a grin. "Aye, you'll be last to fight. The public is going daft over you. We have wagers flying in at all of our locations."

"Did I have another payout from last eve? He said you'd have more for me." He motioned toward the other man.

Blair tossed him a small bag of coin. "Do the same tonight and I'll give you three times that."

"I want the big money after this eve. You told me you'd send me if I won two fights."

Blair guffawed. "True, but I did not expect you to win. I thought you'd get your arse kicked. But you have no fear, do you? I like the look you've taken on—all dressed in black, unshaven, hair a mess. It serves your image well."

Daniel crossed his arms and stood in front of him. If the bastard even dared to change their terms, he'd have him by the throat in a second, but he knew he had to stay calm.

He had to learn about the channel and about Constance. "Where are you sending me on the morrow?"

"I had thought to make you stay for two more fights, but we can wait a sennight for the rest. I have a problem and I need it taken care of. I think you're the man to handle it."

"What is it?"

Lamont leaned against the table where all the coin was being sorted. "There's a wee problem with my…cargo. I don't want this lass brought into town, but my two worst men are handling her. I want her brought to me, so I'm sending you after her just before dawn. 'Tis the red-haired lass."

"Where?"

"I'll give you instructions later. She's of noble blood, so you're not to touch her. 'Tis verra important that she comes to me unharmed."

"Who is she?" Daniel knew he was pushing for too much information, but he just couldn't stop himself.

"Her name does not matter. She'll get me a much bigger payout than usual, and I don't trust her with the two men who have her in hiding. I want her brought here quickly."

Fortunately, his companion asked the next question. "Why is this lass so important?"

Lamont shrugged his shoulders and turned his attention back to his coin. "I don't know, but there are multiple groups looking for her, and I want to be the one who finds her."

"Why so many?" the judge pressed.

Lamont glared at him. "I. Don't. Know. Leave it be. I'll handle it. All Damien needs to do is go where I tell him and bring her to me as quickly as possible. There are others searching for her, too. The faster we get her in our custody, the better 'twill be for us."

Daniel took his coin and left, catching up with Connor not far from the inn. "I leave early on the morrow. You need to follow me." He told him where they would meet.

"I hope Gavin and Gregor move their arses and get us help."

"Why?"

"Because I found out what the three means…"

"What?" Connor stopped to face Daniel.

"There are three groups chasing Constance."

CHAPTER EIGHTEEN

THE TWO MEN MADE THEIR way down through the cellars. They moved all the way to the end and stopped outside the chamber that wasn't locked but left open. "We searched everywhere, even inside Sona Abbey and the Abbey of Angels. No sign of her anywhere, though I've heard her sire has men looking for her."

The person inside said, "Are you sure you searched the abbey thoroughly? Did you make them talk?"

The man who stood behind the first one began to chuckle. "He slapped the abbess. I've never seen anyone hit a woman of the cloth."

"And?"

The first man said, "And naught. It earned me naught. We searched the cellars, the stables, the chapel, even in between the long row of benches in the chapel. There was no sign of any red-haired lass. Every abbey, every kirk, everywhere."

"Lying bastards. I know she's there. And I want her on that next boat. I'm paying you a bulk of coin for this task, if you'll recall. Go back up north again. If her sire's men find her, then kidnap her from them. I want that girl to suffer. I want her out of Scotland forever. Hire as many men as you need. I'll double your pay. Now go."

The two men traipsed back toward the stairway.

But the last words echoed down the passageway. "And don't come back without her!"

CHAPTER NINETEEN

———◆———

DANIEL SAT IN HIS CORNER of the ring beside Terric, wishing this fight were over so he could go after
Constance. The crowd who'd come to the back chamber
to watch the Devil's Hand fight tonight was massive, larger
than he ever would have guessed. To his surprise, the crowd
began to chant, "Devil, Devil, Devil…"

He was growing in popularity. If not for Constance, he
could envision himself staying here for a time. He'd already
made more coin that he'd ever earned before. Not that he
needed it. His parents gave him whatever he needed, but
he hadn't been home in a while because of the Band of
Cousins. Part of him liked being able to provide for himself. It made him feel independent.

What was he going to do once he found Constance? No
doubt Lamont would send more guards with him. Constance would surely react to seeing him, but he'd have to
find a way to put her off. He couldn't let any of Lamont's
men know they were close.

It would probably kill him, but he'd have to be mean and
nasty to convince her that he wasn't the man she'd thought
him to be. He was glad he'd grown out his beard, and the
bigger mess he could make of his hair, the better off he'd
be. His clothes hadn't been washed in a while either.

Constance would not like that.

Then, somehow, he'd find a way to escape with her. First,
he needed to use Lamont to find her.

He sat on the stool, his leg vibrating with tension. He had no idea who he would be fighting this eve. Nor did it matter. He needed to win. Closing his eyes, he found himself thinking of the giggle of a beautiful lass with red hair and green eyes, her nose wiggling as she laughed. The giggle first, then the wiggle. He nearly smiled at the silly thought, but he squelched it because it wouldn't do for his image. He needed to appear ruthless, and ruthless men did not smile. They certainly did not laugh.

Terric clasped his shoulder. "My lord, 'tis only Ivan you'll be fighting."

Given the way the judge and Lamont had spoken about this fight, Daniel had expected a harder challenge. He'd easily beat Ivan before. A few moments later, he understood. Out came another fighter who sat on a stool not far from Ivan. Deathstalker would also be his opponent, apparently.

Terric gulped. "You're to fight two of them at once?" The fear in the lad's face humbled Daniel. Somehow it made his own fear more bearable.

He reached over and patted the lad's shoulder. "Have more faith in me."

"But 'tis one against two," he whispered, two fingers held up as evidence while he stared at Daniel's fearsome competition.

"Mayhap 'twill be only one at a time."

"Och, I do hope so."

The judge stood and nodded to Daniel, then Ivan, and they walked over to stand on either side of him as was the custom. A few moments later, after stirring the crowd up for the fight, he swung his hand over his head and the battle commenced.

Daniel didn't have to fight too hard. He could have leveled Ivan with two moves, but he knew the judge would prefer it if the fight continued until after the middle betting time. To his surprise, the judge stood up and waved his arm, and Ivan stepped back, allowing Deathstalker into the fight.

Deathstalker was no challenge either. Before he knew it, it was the middle of the fight and the men hurried out of the chamber to place more bets. While they were leaving, the judge caught everyone's attention by announcing, "The last battle will be Ivan and Deathstalker together against Devil's Hand."

Terric shot a frightened look at Daniel, who just stood up and flexed his muscles for show.

"Do not worry, Terric. If I must go down, two against one is the way to go." He said those words to calm his new friend, though in truth, he knew he had to be strong. He could not succumb, or he would risk losing his only chance to find his bluebell.

The next round started and Ivan and Deathstalker both jumped at Daniel, who side-stepped them so quickly they banged their heads together. The crowd went into a wild frenzy, which fueled Daniel even more.

He took more punches than he usually did because one would get behind him and try to hold him in place while the other swung at him, but after a while, he tired of this game and went for a different strategy.

In fact, he'd had enough of the whole event. Seeing his chance, he came to an abrupt stop in front of the two of them, shifted his arms down low with a deep growl, and then blasted each of them with a swift elbow under the chin.

The growl received such a reaction that he used it a few more times before he finished the two of them off—one with a fist to his temple and the second with a foot to his midsection that threw him against the back stone wall, knocking him out.

The crowd roared to life as the judge congratulated him and declared him the winner. All he could do was fall onto the stool, while Terric, thankfully, threw water on his face and gave him cups of water and ale, wiping the blood from his face and his fist.

"Well done, my lord," Terric said, a proud grin on his face.

"Terric, you need not call me my lord."

"Only a lord would fight like that. 'Twas amazing to watch."

Daniel patted the lad on the back, then collected his coin from the judge. To his surprise, Lamont had joined him in the large chamber.

"Where to?" Daniel asked him, raising a brow.

Lamont said, "Be outside an hour before the sun rises, and I'll give you complete instructions."

———◆———

DANIEL ROSE EARLY, SPOKE BRIEFLY to Connor to let him know he was leaving. Connor was to follow him, as they'd discussed, and if he had the chance, Daniel planned to search him out to reveal their destination. Lamont had told him he was sending guards with him, but he had no idea how many.

He met Terric along the way to The Hound and Stag. "Greetings, my lord. Good journey to you!"

"Here's enough coin for you to sleep in the inn until I get back." He tossed the lad several coins. He thought for a moment, then added, "Lad, will you take these two bags of coin and hide them for me? I'll come back for them at a later time. If you need any coin, you're welcome to what's inside, but I promise to come back." It would be dangerous to travel with so much coin. He trusted Terric to look after it for him, and if Daniel could not return, the lad would at least be provided for. "Lad, I speak the truth. Consider a coin or two pay for guarding my winnings."

"You gave me plenty. I can eat, too," he said, fingering the coins in the palm of his hand. "Probably for a moon with this much. Many thanks to you, Damien. Godspeed, and I hope we meet upon your return. I'll hide the bags where no one will find them. I promise."

Daniel stopped, turned to his new friend. "Is there any particular reason you remain in Edinburgh, lad?"

The lad stared at the ground. "Nay, 'tis all I know."

Daniel nodded and headed back toward The Hound and the Stag. "I'll look for you the next time I return." He made a mental note to make good on his word as he watched the lad run off to hide his bounty.

Blair Lamont met him outside the inn and led him to the town stables. Four guards stood out front, clearly awaiting someone. "I tried to hire five, but all I could find is four." He moved closer to Daniel so he wouldn't be overheard by the men. "My usual men are unavailable. Many of the guards for hire were out on another mission. My guess is there's another force after the lass. Be aware of your surroundings. My two men, Malcolm and his brother, have her at the waterfall northwest of here, two hours out. I told them to stay away from Edinburgh. Bring her to me right away. No stops. If she arrives safely, and untouched, I'll double the amount I offered. I've doubled the guards' pay so they'll not leave you if there's a whisper of trouble."

Daniel glanced over his shoulder at the goons Lamont had hired. Two carried swords, two carried bows, though he knew their skills were no match for his cousins'. How he prayed they'd be on their way. If he was right, and three separate groups were indeed after Constance, he'd need all the help he could get.

He nodded and retrieved his own horse.

"You better return by nightfall or I'll tell my superior to send his men after you. And you won't like how they fight."

"Your superior? You mean the judge? Or someone else?" Daniel bit his lip, hoping he was about to hear the name of the man who was above Blair Lamont. Could this be the Englishman who was in charge of the entire channel?

"The man who gives me instructions. You'll never meet him."

Daniel forced himself not to react. He'd find out which bastard led the group. He and his cousins had vowed to take them all down: Lamont, his superior, the men who carried the cargo, and the men who kidnapped the cargo. It took many unsavory characters to keep this channel running. One break in the chain could finish the entire operation.

Daniel noticed Terric had returned and stood on the opposite side of the street watching.

"I'll find her." Daniel mounted his destrier in one swift move, putting on a show for the men in the streets watching them. Wherever he went, he caught people staring at him. Even in Edinburgh, word traveled fast. His reputation had to be bigger than he'd guessed.

That gave him second thoughts about the journey he was about to take with four men he didn't know. True, Connor would follow, but perhaps he would do well to enlist the help of another trusted friend. Instead of leaving, he made his way over to Terric. "Do you think you can keep up, lad? I need you along if you can."

"Aye, I can keep up. I have my own dagger, too."

He hopped down. "I'll pay you more to come along." In an undertone, he added, "If anything happens, I want you to find my friend and tell him. He'll be following us at a distance. He's the one who's been at the matches, tall and big with dark hair."

The lad nodded, so Daniel spoke to the four guards, then strode over to the stables and paid for another horse. "Mount up, lad." He turned to the guards and said, "We leave now." The men waited for him to lead the way.

Once they headed out together, passersby began to make comments.

"Look, 'tis Devil's Hand."

A few lads even chased him out of Edinburgh, following

as far as they could. He growled a few times just for show. Then he focused on his mission.

He wouldn't return until he saved his bluebell.

CHAPTER TWENTY

———◆———

CONSTANCE LIFTED HER HEAD FROM the grass, her head still pounding from the fist she'd taken to her jaw last eve. She'd tried again to escape but failed miserably, earning herself a yank on her hair, a slobbery kiss, a paw to her breasts, and a fist to her jaw.

Would she ever be free of these nasty men?

Malcolm was up and leaving a stream of water not far behind her, the sound making her cringe. His brother followed him and said, "Want to watch, lass?" Then he guffawed as if he often did, laughing at his own foul jests.

It struck her that they were both busy, so she pushed herself to a sitting position, pushing past the pain from the raw wounds on her bound wrists. She was about to stand up when Malcolm's voice called to her. "Don't even think about it. We've made it this long. I'll never let you go now."

She fell back down onto the ground with an unladylike grunt.

"Malcolm, when are the others coming? I'm tired of staying here. Why should it matter that there's a waterfall?"

"I told you. They'll be here before the sun is highest, then we'll get our coin and I'll take you to the brothel." Malcolm scratched himself as he meandered back into the clearing. He reached for an oatcake and handed it to her, using the same hand he'd just used to scratch himself under his plaid.

Constance leaned backward, not wanting to get any

closer to that hand.

"Fine. Go hungry."

She got up and they untied her long enough for her to go behind a bush, but then Malcolm moved to bind her hands again. The sound of horses reached their ears before Malcolm finished his job.

He and his brother both ran toward their horses, so she took this as an opportunity from God.

She ran.

———◆———

DANIEL WOULD HAVE TO DO his best to hide his identity. His beard had grown so much since he'd last seen Constance, plus his face was bruised and his hair unclean and unkempt. He suspected she'd have to look at him twice before she recognized him.

Hopefully, it would give him enough time to give her some sort of message.

As soon as they approached the waterfall, they ran into a small group of reivers. He took off toward the thieves, using his sword to cut two of the men down, and left the rest for the guards.

Something else had caught his attention. Two men were headed straight for them from behind a copse of trees, and they looked like the ones Lamont had described.

But he also caught a glimpse of red hair off to the side.

Constance was on the run.

He bellowed to the pair and pointed at them with his sword. "Do not move."

He took off after Constance, planning to lift her onto his horse and leave the others behind, if they were fool enough not to follow him.

The sounds of horses' hooves behind him told him he wouldn't be so fortunate. He'd find another time to steal away. He followed her, listening to the snap of twigs and the rustle of leaves from her feet as he drew close. There was only room for him to pass her on the right, so he would have to use his left arm to grab her. He could only hope she'd hang on to him and not fight him. If she fought hard enough, *Treun* could come off.

He was almost upon her when she glanced over her shoulder and slowed, which gave him the angle he needed. He leaned over and scooped her up, ignoring her squeals as she faltered in his arms.

"Constance, grab my neck."

She stared at him and did as she was instructed, hugging him with delight, but she quickly leaned back and wriggled her nose. "Daniel? 'Tis truly you?"

"Hush. Play along or they'll kill us. I'll explain later."

"Daniel?"

"You don't know me." He turned around and headed back toward the clearing, surprised to see two of the guards right behind him. If he'd tried to run, he wouldn't have made it.

When he got there, he lowered Constance down from his horse with a snarl and a growl. "Don't move, you stupid bitch."

Constance spun around in a fury. If he'd been within reach, she'd have slapped him.

At least he'd had a wee chance to warn her.

He turned his head so the others couldn't see him. Then he smiled and winked, just for her.

She picked up a clump of dirt and threw it at him.

CONSTANCE COULDN'T BELIEVE HER EYES, nor her luck.

At least, she thought it was luck.

A brute on horseback had chased her down. Glancing over her shoulder, she'd feared she'd see Malcolm's brother.

It wasn't Malcolm or his brother. In fact, her pursuer looked distinctly like a bedraggled Daniel.

Her Daniel.

She turned around to face him just before he scooped her up with his amputated arm. She knew it because she could feel something hard at the end, but it wasn't flesh. Other than that surprise, she was ecstatic.

"Daniel?" She wished to hug him and kiss him and jump up and down, but when she saw the expression on his face, something told her not to be effusive in her greeting.

"Hush, play along or they'll kill us."

What was he talking about? She glanced behind him and saw two strange men chasing them. She didn't recognize either one of them.

"You don't know me," he ground out.

What was he talking about? Then it dawned on her. Perhaps he had made his way into a bad group of men just to find her. She'd have to be quiet and see what she could find out.

They reached the clearing, and he dropped her off his horse as if she were no better than a sack of oats.

"Don't move, you stupid bitch."

Well, hellfire, he didn't have to speak to her like that, no matter what he was hiding. Then he had the gall to smile and wink as if she were in on the joke. She picked up a clump of dirt and threw it at him.

She reminded herself that this was her Daniel. He had an odd sense of humor, certainly, but he was born a Drummond and had the heart of a Highlander.

She backed away toward a tree at the corner of the clearing, noticing Malcolm hadn't properly secured her hands. She could free them if she so wished. Ignoring her captors—Daniel could take care of them—she sat and leaned against the tree, setting her bound hands in her lap where the men wouldn't see the dangling ends of the rope.

Malcolm yelled, "Who the hell are you?"

"Damien. Lamont sent me." He climbed off his horse and crossed the clearing, standing in front of the two brothers. His expression told her he intended to intimidate them, and the look on Malcolm's face told her he was succeeding. True, Daniel wasn't as tall or as broad as some of his cousins, but he still wasn't afraid of any of these fools.

Damien? Her hunch had been right. Daniel was hiding his identity.

Malcolm swallowed. "Give me my coin and we'll leave. You can have the wench. She's done naught but cause me trouble. She kicked me and bruised my leg."

Daniel snorted. "Looks like she got worse than she gave." He moved over and bent down, lifting her chin so he could look at the bruises on her face. She did her part and shoved his hand away.

Daniel didn't hesitate. He strode over to Malcolm, hauled his fist back, and punched him in the jaw. "Lamont said she was not to be touched."

"I didn't touch her."

"Then why does she have two bruises on her face?"

"She fell."

Malcolm's brother broke into a gale of laughter.

Daniel strode over to him and gripped him by the tunic. "Did *you* touch her?" he growled.

"Nay, nay! I didn't touch her. I wanted to, but he wouldn't allow it." He pointed to his brother.

Daniel set him down and said, "You got your coin. Move on. You'll only slow us down."

"He promised me more," Malcolm said, his tone verging on a whine.

"Then take it up with him. He's still in Edinburgh. Go see what more he'll give you."

The two moved toward their horses while Daniel went to chat with the guards he brought with him.

It gave her the chance to look him over.

Daniel looked like hell. His hair looked like it hadn't been combed in a moon. His beard was the same. In fact, she couldn't believe Daniel could have grown such a full beard in that short time. His face and clothes were dirty, and he sported several of his own bruises and a black eye.

What had happened to him? She was quite certain he wasn't with any of his cousins.

Before she had time to give it anymore thought, a young lad emerged from behind some bushes. Another person she'd never seen before.

Daniel turned to the lad and said, "Terric, get the lass some water and a piece of cheese from my saddlebag."

The lad, Terric, quickly did as he was bid, handing her the cheese and a skin of water. He untied her hands so she could eat and gave her a linen square to wash with. "Sorry, but 'tis the best I have, my lady. Is there water nearby?"

She pointed in the direction of the waterfall, and he took off, but then he returned to whisper. "Dinnae worry. Damien will not hurt you. He's the best fighter in all of Edinburgh. They call him Devil's Hand. But he'd not hurt a lass."

Constance washed her hands and face, then nibbled on the small piece of cheese. How long had it been since she had eaten? She watched Daniel, his broad shoulders, his lean waist. She thought his shoulders had grown wider, if that were possible. He gave curt instructions to the guards, informing them they had ten minutes to take care of their needs.

Terric returned to her side, and something about him caught her attention. "Lad, what happened to your hand?"

"I was born like this."

Daniel came over and nodded. "Ten minutes and we leave."

She looked at his arm and asked, "What is that thing you have on?"

Terric quickly stepped in to defend Daniel. "Damien doesn't have a hand either. We're the same 'cept I never had one and he lost his."

Though she couldn't reveal she knew him, she thought

it fair to press him about the contraption on his left arm. "What is that creation you have where you left hand should be?" She lifted her gaze to his and was instantly lost in those forest green eyes.

Daniel held his left arm up for her to see. "My cousin crafted this for me, and Terric here helped me perfect it."

"Do you like it?"

He gave her an unreadable look. "Of course, I like it. I don't have to walk around and have people stare at my stub anymore. Lass, if you need to take care of your needs, Terric will guard you. We leave in ten minutes."

"Where are you taking me?"

"To Edinburgh."

"What for?" She tried to gauge Daniel's meaning by searching his face, but he gave away nothing.

"I was hired to retrieve a red-haired lass and bring her to Edinburgh. 'Tis all I know. I bring you there and collect my coin. Where you go after that, I have no idea." He spun on his heel and strode away without giving her even a hint of what the truth could be.

Unless he'd just told her the truth.

CHAPTER TWENTY-ONE

———•———

GOD'S BONES, BUT HE HAD to stop looking into his bluebell's mesmerizing eyes. He'd missed her terribly—he hadn't realized how much until he actually had her in his arms again.

Now he just had to convince his feisty lass to trust him. He would get her away from Lamont and all the others. Then he'd propose to her. She'd see how powerful he was with his new arm.

She'd know he had the strength to protect her.

He waited until she returned from the bushes, then ushered her over to his horse.

One of Lamont's guards said, "Give her to me. Then I'll not worry that you'll take off with her."

"She rides with me." Daniel didn't even look at the arse. As if he would allow anyone else to touch his sweet bluebell.

"Nay. I want her. 'Tis the best way. How do I know you'll not just run away with her to collect the money yourself?" the guard persisted, his eyes narrowing at him.

Daniel returned the narrowed gaze. *Try touching her and see how fast you die.*

"Lamont put me in charge, so she stays with me. Unless you care to fight me for the honor." He grabbed Constance by the waist and hoisted her up onto his horse. To his surprise, she almost flew off the other side. Hell, but she'd be blistering his ear later. His muscle mass must have grown from all the fighting. He hadn't intended to be so forceful.

To his surprise, the other guard dismounted and came toward him, brandishing his sword. Daniel pulled his own weapon out of its sheath and defended himself against the attack, knocking the blade out of his hand with ease. He stared at the lout, but the big brute didn't back down. Daniel sighed, wishing it hadn't come to this. After all the fighting he'd done, he'd make short work of this fool.

Daniel dropped his weapon to the ground. "We don't have time for this. I'll give you one chance to back down." When the fool swaggered forward instead, Daniel reached for his collar, tugged him closer to strike him in the jaw, and then threw three quick punches to his belly. While the guard leaned forward, moaning, he lifted the man over his head and tossed him into the bushes.

"Now can we take our leave?" he asked, as he moved over to pick up his sword. No one responded, so he mounted behind Constance. Terric prepared to leave, a wide grin on his face, and the rest of the men followed suit. Daniel gave the fool who was still flat on his back a few minutes to get up, then flicked the reins of his horse and led the way back toward Edinburgh.

They'd only been gone about an hour when the sound of approaching riders reached their ears. He motioned for his men to move off the main path, with the idea of allowing the group to move past them, but unfortunately, it was not to be.

One man set his gaze on Constance and bellowed, "There she is! He has the red-haired lass. Get her!"

Chaos ensued as the men did battle. Daniel found a copse of trees to set Constance down safely, then returned to the fray. His group of six, including Terric, was up against a dozen men. He fought for a short while, then realized he should take advantage of this situation.

True, he'd felled three men on his own, but two of Lamont's men had also gone down, so he knew he needed to make a decision quickly. He said to Terric, "Remember what I told you. Find Connor."

Terric didn't hesitate—he took off while Daniel reached down for Constance and tossed her up in front of him. He then pulled on the reins to send his horse off into the woods on a gallop.

"Duck," he said to her. Branches were flying by faster than he'd like, but with no alternative, he just had to protect both their faces.

"Daniel, where are you taking me?"

"Hush. There are still at least eight men bent on chasing us with only two Lamont guards left, so 'twas time to take our leave. I'll answer all your questions as soon as we get away."

Constance squealed as she ducked from another branch that still managed to hit her in the back of her head. He found a different path and set his horse into a heavy gallop once they found a meadow.

His horse was far more powerful that any beast the reivers would have, so he hoped to outrun them. He pushed Constance forward and leaned over her in an effort to protect her from whatever might come their way. It wasn't comfortable, but it was efficient.

Six men chased them for a few hours, but none of their mounts were a match for his destrier. They dropped off one at a time over the next hour until he saw no one behind them. Their brisk pace kept them from chattering much, though he was able to squeeze her waist a couple of times. Once they reached smoother ground, he whispered, "I missed you, lass."

She spun around to stare at him. "Daniel, my thanks for coming for me. Where were they taking me?"

"Lass, I'd love to explain all, but there are three groups after you, so we must make haste." He kissed her temple and she turned back around, clutching his forearm as they continued through the forest at an exhausting pace.

They encountered another group of men on horseback, who set after them as soon as they caught sight of Constance, and all he could do was curse and growl. "Is the entire Highlands after you, bluebell?"

He didn't dare slow down until it was nearly nightfall and they were halfway to Drummond land. They hadn't run into another horseman for a few hours, and he knew there was a cave up ahead, although his horse wouldn't fit. If the weather turned bad, he could protect her from freezing until he got her to Castle Drummond for safety.

He'd hoped to catch sight of Connor or Terric, or mayhap even his other cousins, but every person they'd encountered thus far had been an enemy. The cave was situated behind a small waterfall. He dismounted, leaving his panting horse by the water for a drink, and helped her down.

"Sorry, Constance. I know 'twas a rough ride, but I had to get you away quickly."

She threw her arms around his neck and buried her face into his shoulder. "My thanks for getting me away from them. Why were they taking me to Edinburgh? What is going on? Why do they all want me?" Tears slid down her cheeks. He took her hand gently and guided her behind the waterfall, removing his tunic and her mantle so they could wash.

"Here, throw some cool water on your face. You're as covered with dirt as I am."

She allowed him to wash her face and her neck, wiping the tears and the grime away, before she repeated her question. "Why, Daniel? Why is this happening?"

"I believe 'tis the gemstone. Everyone wants it. My guess is your sire has put out a bounty for someone to find you and the stone. The reivers have also caught wind of it, likely because someone saw it at the abbey and tongues started wagging. They have no guilt. They'll do anything to get that stone, so when I heard about it in Edinburgh, I had to step in."

"Why were you in Edinburgh? Were you not with your cousins?"

"Aye, we were searching for information about the underground, hoping it would lead us to the Channel of Dubh, and it did. But the red-haired lass consumed everyone's attention. When I heard about you, we sent Gavin and Gregor back to get help. Connor should be behind me by a couple of hours." He reached over and tucked a mass of stray curls back behind her ear. The ride had made a mess of her plaited hair, though she'd never looked more beautiful to him. "Everyone wants you, my sweet bluebell, so why are you not safely in the abbey?"

She tipped her head over and drank from the waterfall, then plopped down on a stone at the mouth of the cave. Her tears had finally stopped.

She took a big, shuddering breath and said, "I left the abbey because my presence there was putting them at risk. Two different groups came looking for me. I'm quite sure one of the groups was sent by my sire. The other men were ruthless, and one even slapped the mother abbess. The nuns had just moved a group of wee lassies to the abbey, all under ten summers, and I was afraid the men would hurt them."

"So how did you end up with those two fools?" He replaced his tunic, then moved over to sit beside her, settling her mantle over her shoulders to ensure she was warm.

"I set out at night, hoping to make it to Muir Castle before dawn. From there, I hoped one of your cousins would help me get to Grant Castle to see Rose. But those two daft men caught me an hour from the castle. So what now?"

"Now, we rest. I expect Connor will be here shortly. And please don't call me Daniel. We have to keep the ruse up if they return, and 'twill be easier if we practice."

"Who is Damien? Why are you all bruised?"

"Because I've been fighting for coin, and I've won a lot of bouts."

"Why?"

He plunked down next to her and leaned back on his elbows. "'Tis a long story and I'm tired. Can we not rest before I tell you?" He reached out to pluck a few weeds and leaves from her clothing. She looked as though she'd been through hell, and he knew he fared no better. "I need a couple of hours of sleep, and I suspect you have not slept well of late either. Connor should be here by then and the rest of my cousins fast behind him. Then we'll take you to Drummond land and decide what to do next."

"How will Connor know we're here?"

"We discussed it beforehand. This is where Finlay took his sister when she was near death. He knows it well. We all do. If we move back inside, we can sleep and my horse will awaken me when someone arrives."

"But 'tis cold in here."

"I'd be happy to be of service." He waggled his brow at her.

"You will not touch me," she said, words burbling out of her like water in a spring. "Not out here. Not where you can run away and leave me. Not where…"

The hurt in her words told her there was a story there, but he'd not press her for it now. Daniel put his finger to her lips to silence her, then stood and held his hand out to her. "I'll not defile you, I promise. In fact, I'm sneaking out to bathe under the waterfall quickly or you'll never kiss me again."

He left, giving her some time alone while he doused himself under the waterfall. A bit of cold would help keep his desire for his sweet lass in check, or so he hoped.

Once he finished, he came back inside the cave, surprised to see her sitting with her back against the stone wall, nearly asleep. She heard his footsteps and jumped up, her eyes wide. The poor lass must be exhausted. He found a place where he could put his extra plaid down for her, though she insisted on being at least an arm's length from him. She finally curled up in a spot facing away from him. Though he intended to leave her alone, he soon heard her tossing to get comfortable. He rolled over with a growl, lifting her and tucking her in close, then gave her his upper arm to sleep on.

She sighed and fell asleep in an instant.

CHAPTER TWENTY-TWO

———

CONSTANCE WOKE UP IN THE dark, alarmed because she felt something tickling her cheek. Her hand moved up to her face. There was naught there, but then she swore there was a creature at her neck. A mouse? A rat? What the hell could it be?

Suddenly, it dawned on her where she was and what was bothering her. Grabbing the dagger out of her boot, she sat up and spun around on her arse. Then, leaning down over Daniel, she placed her knife at his throat. She'd had all she could take, and she would fix this now.

Daniel's eyes flew open. "Hellfire! Do you always threaten the man who loves you by holding a dagger at his throat?" His gaze was wide-eyed, but he didn't move a muscle.

"Stay just like that and I won't hurt you." She took hold of one side of his beard and sliced a huge piece of it off with her dagger.

"What the hell are you doing?" His hand flew up to protect his face.

"I've had enough. I don't like your beard," She hissed as she reached for the other side and managed to cut a hunk of it off before he moved back.

"Leave me be, woman. I like my beard." He scuttled away from her, but she wouldn't stop. He was nearly out of the cave, but she followed him.

"I don't like that long, itchy thing. I thought I had a mouse at the back of my neck. And I don't like that mess

on your head either. I'll comb it before some critter starts
to live in it." She reached for a hunk of his hair, but he
bolted to his feet, backing away from her.

"What has happened to you?" He stared at her, wide-
eyed, his hands protecting his face.

"Naught has happened to me. What has happened to
you? I don't like your beard and I don't like your unkempt
hair." She stowed her dagger away and crossed her arms as
she stared at him.

He said, "I'll shave when I get back home, but this is part
of my new image. Leave it for now."

"Well, I don't like your new image. It doesn't suit you. It
makes you look like one of *them*." She reached for his arm
and tugged at the loop around his shoulder. "I don't like
this thing either. Give it to me."

He tried to hang on to the contraption, but she managed
to tug it away. After giving it a brief glance, she threw it
behind her. Her Daniel's scars were part of him, and she'd
just as soon see them.

"Constance, God's bones, would you leave me be? What's
gotten into you?" He stepped back until he was nearly
under the waterfall.

"What's gotten into me? You. Your hair is a mess, your
beard is disgusting, you have some strange device attached
to your arm. Your face is all bruised and you have a black
eye. Your clothes are filthy. I barely recognized you. I
understand that you went to Edinburgh to help find the
Channel of Dubh, but why have you changed *everything*
about you?" She kept moving closer, and her tone dropped
so low she could barely get her words out. "What have you
done with my sweet, loving Daniel Drummond, *Damien*?
I prefer you the way you were."

"Don't throw my new hand away." He made his way
around her to retrieve it. "My cousin worked verra hard on
that, and I just fashioned it the way I liked it." He grabbed
it, then stood with his legs braced and his arms crossed in

front of him. "I like it. It makes me different."

"I don't like you different. And I don't like your new name either. Or the way you growl like a wild animal. What is that?" She pushed her finger at his chest. "I loved my Daniel exactly as he was. Hair and dirt and wild sounds and strange names and…what else don't I know?"

His eyes glittered, and she frowned, realizing she'd just admitted her love for him, but then it registered that *he* had admitted his love for her first. "Wait. You said, 'the man who loves you.'"

"Nay, I said, 'the man you love.'"

"Nay, you did not. I recall it distinctly. You said, 'the man who loves you.'"

He growled, a low growl that she suspected he'd done just for effect. "Fine. I love you, or I did. But mayhap not anymore. You've turned daft."

"You've made me daft. How long have you known you love me?"

He barked out a laugh, though it sounded a wee bit bitter. "I don't know. Mayhap sometime back in the abbey? Probably started when you first asked me about my arm. I pretended I hadn't noticed it was gone, and you laughed instead of looking shocked and embarrassed. You didn't pity me."

"Why didn't you tell me?"

"Because you didn't want me. I couldn't protect you, and you knew it. I let you fall down the stairs because I only had one hand. Well, I can protect you now. I have a reputation as one of the fiercest fighters in Edinburgh, and they call me Devil's Hand. I'm keeping the hand."

"Oh, Daniel." Stunned by this admission, she was suddenly speechless. She ran to him and wrapped her arms around his waist, forcing him to drop his still crossed arms. "It wasn't because of you that I left. That had naught to do with it."

He remained stiff for a moment, but then he settled his

chin on the top of her head and held her close. "Then why did you leave? I thought we had something, and all of a sudden, you couldn't get away from me fast enough. You ran back to the abbey and hardly spoke to me. Why?"

"Those men were after me, Daniel. I couldn't put your clan at risk. I knew my sire wouldn't stop searching for me. I knew he intended to make me pay for my transgression, and then I'd have to leave you. Besides, you didn't know the truth…"

"Then tell me the truth now." He loosened his grip and lifted her chin.

She stepped back and moved toward the front of the cave, staring out at the waterfall, its sound mesmerizing her. There was no sense in trying to keep her secret any longer. Hugging herself against the chill in the air, she decided it was time to be honest.

"My sire is Baron Douglas Lockhart of Lee in Lanark-shire. I stole my mother's gemstone because I loved her so much, I wanted a memory of her. I don't plan to ever return."

Daniel came up behind her and leaned his chin on her shoulder. "I take it you weren't sent away because your seven siblings were starving?"

She glanced down at him and gave him a wry smile. "Nay. We are far from starving, but I do have seven sib-lings. I ran away because I made a big mistake and my sire was furious, so furious that he promised to put me on an island alone for the rest of my life, among other things. And that is the reason I left you." She stepped away from him so she could face him. It was time for her to tell him everything. "I knew you wouldn't be allowed to marry me, even if I were lucky enough for you to ask. I love being with you—no one has ever made me laugh the way you do—but when the men came to Muir Castle, I knew my sire wouldn't give up. He'd make me pay, and he'd sooner drag me away from you than risk revealing my secret. I…I cannot marry." She stared at him, hoping he would guess the reason a lass of noble blood would be taken out of the marriage mart, so to speak.

But Daniel still looked confused. "There is naught you could tell me that would change my mind." He reached for her cheek, touching his finger to the tear that had just slid down her cheek and lifting it to his tongue, tasting it. "I love you, Constance Lockhart of Lee, Lanarkshire, even the salt of your tears. Naught you could tell me would make me change my mind."

She placed her hand on his chest and he covered it with his one hand. Staring at their entwined hands, she continued, "I fancied a local lad who I thought was from the next castle, and I let him talk me into giving away my maidenhead. I'm no longer a virgin, Daniel, so no man will want me. The lad was only a local stable lad, and he bragged about his accomplishment to all who would listen. My sire was so furious he told our steward to get the boat ready, he planned to take me to a deserted island in the morn and leave me there. So I ran away."

He lifted her fingertips to his lips, kissing each one. "And you thought that would keep me from loving you and wanting you?"

He did not even pause to think about it. His response was immediate, his love unconditional.

The tears blossomed again, and she was powerless to stop them. "Oh, Daniel. I do love you." He wrapped her in his embrace and she cried into his shoulder, something she had needed to do. "No one wants a lass who doesn't have her maidenhead," she said through her tears, "and if my sire ever finds me, he'll still leave me on the deserted island. I'll die there a spinster."

"*This* man wants you, and I don't care if you lost your maidenhead. 'Tis just a piece of skin. And if we decide to marry, Baron Douglas Lockhart couldn't do a thing." He ran his hand down her back, being his usual tender self.

"Marry? You want to marry me? After hearing all that, you would still consider marrying me?" She stepped back to bring her gaze to his, swiping the tears away.

"I did until you took my arm from me and cut my beard. Look at me. I'm uneven now. I'm a hideous beast."

She tapped his chest, trying to stop herself from giggling. "Daniel, this is no time for teasing. I love you. Do you love me?"

He grasped her hand and tugged her close again, then bent down on one knee.

And her heart nearly burst.

"Constance Lockhart of Lee, Lanarkshire. I love you with all my heart. Will you do me the honor of becoming my wife?"

"Oh Daniel, aye." She fell against him, nearly knocking him over.

"Then we'll get married as soon as we can," he whispered in her ear. "As long as you promise not to throw my new hand away. It can be verra useful, at times."

She chuckled and he sat cross-legged, tugging her onto his lap. She said, "Agreed, as long as you don't take it to bed with you. I don't want it in our bed. And I don't like your new name, I want your old one."

His lips crushed hers in a searing kiss, but he ended it long enough to say, "Agreed."

Then she said, "I think I need to fix your beard. I did make a big mess of it."

He growled, picked her up and settled her so they were lying face to face.

She said, "Now, that growl I like."

CHAPTER TWENTY-THREE

———◆———

DANIEL SAID, "CONSTANCE, I DON'T want to wait. If we pass a kirk, I wish to marry you now."

She nibbled his ear lobe and whispered, "I agree. Make me yours now, Daniel, and we'll marry as soon as we find a priest."

Daniel wanted nothing more than to make her his, but wouldn't he be just as guilty as the other lad who took advantage of her? A noise from outside interrupted his carnal thoughts and he pushed himself to his feet, moving outside to see what had caused the sound.

He'd grabbed *Treun* just in case he needed it, fear of Lamont's men and Baron Lockhart's guards always at the forefront of his mind. There was no one around, of that he was certain. His horse still munched away at a cluster of tall grasses. The area was well hidden, so he doubted they'd be bothered. Connor would use his bird call to apprise him of his arrival.

He could understand why Constance had been shocked at his appearance. Though his heart was the same, he had new confidence. No longer the man with the stub, he felt more qualified to fight as a guard.

He turned around and headed back toward the waterfall—and then stopped short. Constance stood in front of him, her hands folded in front of her.

"Did you find anyone?"

"Nay. We're quite alone. 'Tis a very isolated cave."

"Good," she said, reaching up to untie the ribbon on her gown. She lifted it over her head and tossed it aside, then lowered her shift, finally standing before him with naught on.

Daniel's mouth went dry as he took in her beauty. "Constance, you are the most beautiful thing I've ever seen." He strode over to her, clutching one of her hands as he kissed her lips. "Are you verra certain, my wee one?" he asked. Then he took *Treun* and tossed it down next to her gown on the leaves of the forest.

"Aye, I've never been as certain as I am now. Make me yours, Daniel. I wish to lie together as husband and wife."

Daniel let go of her hand and raced over to his horse, pulling a Drummond plaid out from his saddle bag. He returned, unfolded it, and said, "'Tis the best I have, but 'twill work."

He took her hand in his and draped the end of the plaid over both of their wrists. "Constance Lockhart of Lee, I pledge my troth to you. I promise to love and protect you forever, and I promise to wed you as soon as we are able to locate a priest and a kirk."

He nodded to her, smiling at the happy tears he saw in her eyes. "Your turn, lass," he whispered.

"Daniel Drummond, I promise to love you forever, and I pledge my troth to you until we are able to find a kirk and a priest."

He settled the plaid on the ground over a soft bed of leaves and removed his boots and his trews. When she shivered, he wrapped his arm around her. "I promise to keep you warm." He led her to the plaid and helped her get comfortable on it before he lay next to her on his side, staring into her eyes. "Do you trust me, lass? I'll not hurt you."

"But it hurt before."

Daniel reached up and wiped the tear from her cheek. "'Tis a common occurrence the first time for a lass. I will make sure you are ready for me. In fact, 'tis the perfect place for us to lie together the first time because you'll not be embarrassed when you scream my name from pleasure."

She giggled. "Daniel, I love you, but I don't think I'll scream your name. Please do not be upset if I don't. It doesn't mean I don't love you."

He leaned toward her to give her his heat, his hand roaming down her back and across her soft bottom, not once, not twice, but three times—until she squirmed next to him. Each time he slowed his caress a bit more. "Nay, I won't be upset. But I think you will do it. Just wait and see."

How he hoped he was telling the truth. He wasn't as experienced as many others he knew. With his hand the way it was, he hadn't gained the interest of many lasses. But he had listened attentively to his cousins and learned all he could, swearing that when the day came, he would know how to make his love call his name.

He kissed her, a soft kiss to ease her into the passion he had already sensed in his bluebell, just waiting to be brought to the surface. One of the things he loved most about Constance was how open she was with her feelings.

She sighed and reached up to the back of his neck, wrapping her hands there, so he deepened the kiss, angling his mouth over hers until they reached a rhythm together, dueling tongues as they both became breathless.

"Daniel, I've never known a kiss to be so wonderful."

He chuckled, trailing kisses down her neck, taking time to focus on the fine bone on her chest. His hand reached down to cup her breast, massaging the pert mound and then rubbing the taut peak until she bucked against him.

"Daniel!"

He leaned down to take her nipple in his mouth, breathing over the sensitive apex and whispering, "Not loud enough, love." He suckled her, teasing her with his tongue until she gripped his hair, tugging him closer. His hand traced a path down her hip, across her bottom again until he reached her core. Parting her folds, he slipped his fingertip inside her, growling with delight when he found she was slick with need. He kissed her again, slanting his mouth over hers so he could go deeper. His hand continued to stroke her until she parted her legs for him.

He leaned on his elbow and held himself above her, taking himself in his hand and saying, "Constance, touch me. I want you to know exactly what you do to me."

She opened her eyes and touched him, pulling her hand back quickly and glancing at him. "I don't know what to do."

He guided her hand and said, "Stroke me the way I stroke you."

She did so with a tentative grip, testing him, moving her hand back and forth until he could take no more.

"Lass, I cannot wait or I'll spend myself before we even start." He slid his knee between her thighs. "Guide me in," he said, his voice husky with passion. "Open for me."

He touched the tip to her opening. She gasped with pleasure, her legs spreading wider for him, and he thrust inside her, stopping for just a moment to ask, "Lass, I'm not hurting you…"

"Nay, Daniel. More, I need more. I don't know what…"

Daniel plunged into her, pleased to see how quickly she caught his rhythm, and gripped her hip to hold her while he continued to thrust her at an angle she seemed to enjoy. He drove into her and began to lose all sense of what he was doing, the pleasure of her tightness sending him close to the abyss. He was nearly there, but he was determined she would reach her peak with him, so he reached down to touch her in just the right spot, and she yelled, "Daniel!"

They careened into oblivion together, her contractions driving him mad until he called her name with a roar and finished.

When his breathing calmed, he kept his weight on his

elbow, kissed her neck, and said, "I heard my name."

She did her best to even out her breathing but failed. Finally, she said, "True, but you were louder."

Daniel couldn't argue.

CHAPTER TWENTY-FOUR

ANIEL HEARD THE BIRD CALL he'd been expect-
ing about half an hour after they'd dressed and
returned to the cave. "Sorry, love. I have to answer my
cousin. I'm betting 'tis Connor." They'd been snuggled
together, enjoying the peacefulness of the forest and talking
about family.

He kissed her forehead and pushed himself to a standing
position. He left the cave to stand next to the waterfall, his
gaze searching the forest rich with autumn color, but he
saw no one. He echoed the birdcall, and a few moments
later, Connor appeared guiding his horse to the burn,
though Terric wasn't with him.

"You are hale?" Connor asked.

"Aye," Daniel said, glancing over his shoulder as Constance stepped out behind him and peeked over his
shoulder. "Any news?"

Connor waited until he was closer to Daniel and Constance before he spoke to them. "Pleased to see you again,
lass. Those brutes didn't hurt you, did they?"

"Aye, but I took care of everything," Daniel said—just as
Constance answered, "Nay, they did not hurt me."

Daniel quirked a brow at her, pointing to the bruise on
her face, "Fortunately, you cannot see it."

She shrugged. "It does not hurt any longer now that I'm
with you." She leaned against him, and he wrapped his
arm around her.

"Go on. She'll mend," Daniel said.

Connor gave him an odd look. "Did you trim your beard?"

"Nay," Daniel barked.

"I did," Constance replied, giggling. "He looks better, don't you agree?"

"Never mind," Daniel said, squeezing her shoulder lightly. "What have you uncovered? And did you see Terric?"

"Maggie and Will said to meet you at the kirk closest to Drummond land. I sent Terric back to Edinburgh. I had to promise him you would return to see him someday."

"I will. He's a fine lad. Why did Maggie want us to meet them there? Although 'twill suit our needs perfectly." He winked at Constance. "We're going to marry as soon as we can."

"Congratulations, but you might wish to arrive ahead of them. Maggie and Will ran into a baron searching for his red-haired daughter." He glanced at Constance and asked, "Any idea who they could be referring to?"

Constance took a deep breath and whispered, "Baron Lockhart of Lee?"

"That verra one. He's ready to tear half of the Highlands apart to find you. Maggie said she'd lead him to a meeting with you. Your sire, lass?"

"Aye. I'll talk to him, but I'll not go with him."

"I'll go with you," Daniel said calmly, rubbing her shoulder. "I'll ask him for your hand and we'll marry in the kirk. There will be no arguments."

"I hope you're right," she said through a few tears.

"Connor, do you have any food?" Daniel asked as he helped Constance to his horse.

Connor said, "I have some bread for you." He tossed it to Daniel, who handed it directly to Constance.

Connor then tossed him a hunk of cheese, so he broke it in two, giving half to Constance and popping the other half in his mouth. "Are you ready, lass? I promise to stay by your side."

She nodded. "I'll have to face him sometime. Why not now? Though I'm surprised he wishes to meet with us in the middle of the night.

"Maggie is bringing torches."

They headed out, Connor in the lead.

"How far, Daniel?" Constance asked softly.

"Probably two hours. Close your eyes, lass."

She leaned against him but stared straight ahead. "I doubt I could fall asleep knowing I'm going to see my father."

"'Twill all be over soon. Think on it that way. We love each other, we're getting married, and no one will stop us."

She finally turned her head to look at him. "I pray you're right," she said, a twinge of uncertainty in her voice.

IT WASN'T LONG BEFORE THEY arrived at the kirk, though it was past midnight. Several torches had been arranged around the clearing off the path near the church.

Constance's heart was in her throat, mostly because she was afraid of her father and what he would do when he finally saw her. They stayed on their horses because the sound of other horses could be heard in the distance.

Maggie and Will strode out of the kirk, followed by three of Daniel's cousins and several guards. "I wonder where my brother is," Daniel said to Constance, though he did not speak loud enough for the others to hear. "You're trembling, lass. I'll protect you. You are mine now, even though the church has not made it official. We agreed, did we not?"

She turned to gaze into his deep green eyes and whispered, "Aye. We are husband and wife in my eyes."

"Then that is how we shall present it to your sire. We are married. And we will be in the church's eyes by the end of the morrow."

Four of the guards who'd come with Maggie and Will

mounted their horses and rode off, although she had no idea where they were going. Maggie and Will walked toward them. "Constance, your sire is on his way. I promised him you would talk with him. Do you agree to that?"

"Aye, but I'll not go with him. He wished to put me on an island, punish me for…"

Maggie held her hand up. "You need not disclose that. We're going to mount up, but I wanted your agreement first. We will ensure this does not become a battle. Gavin and Gregor are our best archers so I have them positioned out of sight. Braden and Connor will help out as needed." Turning to Daniel, she asked, "Have you any word of lasses being stolen and sent away?"

"Nay, but Blair Lamont manages the Edinburgh part of the Channel of Dubh. Moves lasses at least once a month. They come from the north and his men bring them to the east. We still need to find out where."

"We'll do what we can." The sound of approaching horses grew louder as Maggie asked, "Anyone else we need to worry about?"

Daniel shook his head. "I wouldn't be surprised to see Lamont and his men show up, but there's no one else to my knowledge. We sent some reivers running, and I doubt they'll be back."

Maggie moved over to her horse and Will helped her up. After he mounted, he said, "I'll go to the side of the kirk with Braden. Connor, join me."

"Maggie, where's David?" Daniel asked.

"He returned to your land."

Moments later, the horses came into their view, two banners held up even in the dark of the night. The full moon helped illuminate their view of the approaching men.

In an instant, she knew.

Constance whispered, "'Tis my sire. He's in front in between the guards with the banners. How many men are behind him?"

Daniel whistled. "I'd say about a hundred guards."

"We cannot fight one hundred guards," she said urgently.

"Listen to me," he whispered in her ear. "I'd prefer to keep you in front of me where I know I can protect you, but if you'd rather stay out of sight, I could move you behind me on the horse."

"Nay, I wish to see my sire clearly. I'm done hiding from him, Daniel. Can you not see I must stand for what I believe is right?"

He kissed her forehead when she turned to him. "I support you, but I must insist that if anyone raises a sword or makes a battle cry, I will set you down so you can run to the kirk and hide. Agreed?"

"Aye, and I promise to wait for you." Her gaze settled on the sea of horses, the warriors all tall in their seats, their eyes on her. The old Constance would have melted under her sire's scrutiny, but with Daniel behind her, she had renewed strength and confidence. Her sire no longer held the same kind of power over her.

Maggie brought her horse to stand in front of them, waiting for Baron Lockhart of Lee to come closer. "As promised, I have your daughter here. Do I still have your word you will not attack us?"

"Aye, you have my word. Constance, come here." Her sire's grim face told her all. He wasn't happy to see her, in fact, he looked more furious than ever. "I don't know who you're with, but you'll get rid of that man. You are of noble blood, and he looks as though he's been living on the streets of Edinburgh."

"Papa! Stop being so cruel and judgmental. Daniel saved my life. I'm not coming with you." She could almost see the steam rising from the top of her sire's head. In fact, if she were any closer, she was certain she'd see that narrowed gaze of his that she detested.

With a clenched jaw, he said, "I'm not going home *without* you. Your mother misses you and so do your sisters."

He kept his stiff posture, his chin lifted as if to declare himself superior to everyone around him—that warrior look her mother often bemoaned. Aye, he was angry.

Constance noticed he hadn't said a word about missing her himself. Though she couldn't deny that she wished to see her mother and her siblings, she'd find a way to visit them someday. Surely *they* would be happy to hear she'd married the man she loved.

Her father waited for her to move, but she didn't. He wasn't a patient man, and it didn't take long for him to lose his temper.

"Constance, if I have to dismount and drag you from that horse, I will. I'm telling you for the last time to come here."

"Papa, nay. I'm not going home with you. I…"

Daniel rested his hand on her arm and squeezed it. "Baron, if circumstances were different, I would ask for your daughter's hand in marriage because I love her, but I don't think you'd be agreeable. Whether you agree or not, we are getting married in that kirk. I've asked her and she's accepted. As far as we are concerned, we are a married couple."

Her father's voice came out in a bellow this time. "I will not allow you to marry some man with only one hand. How the hell can he protect you?"

"I just told you that he saved my life. Is that not enough for you?" She bent over her horse to plead with him. Why was her father so obstinate?

"Nay, he's naught but a ruffian. You deserve better. But if you recall, you ruined your chances of a good marriage."

"Papa! Daniel, would you please take me away from here?" She had to leave before she erupted in tears because she would not give her father the satisfaction of seeing her cry.

Her sire unsheathed his sword, which set off a chain reaction all around him. His men wielded their weapons, and so did Daniel and Will and Maggie.

"You gave your word you would not go on the attack, Baron," Maggie cautioned.

"I will gain my daughter back."

Maggie said, "My lord, do you not think she is old enough to make her own decisions? Mayhap you should try talking with her instead of ordering her about."

"Of course that would be your viewpoint. She's my daughter and I own her. 'Tis the way of the world. She'll do as I tell her. I am quite capable of finding her a husband once she has paid the consequences of her poor judgment."

"Papa, I don't want you choosing my husband. I'll choose my own and I want Daniel. He's not a ruffian, he's a Drummond."

"Do not turn to lies to convince me to support this marriage."

A rustling from behind them caught their attention. One group of men came at them from the left side, and another approached from the right. Constance whispered, "Daniel, who are these men?"

Maggie and Will backed their horses up toward the kirk while Maggie spoke to the leader of the group approaching from the left. "You wish to pass? We'll move out of your way."

The man drew his sword and stared at them with a wicked smile on his face. Constance guessed he had about fifty men behind him. She had little experience with counting men, but it appeared to be half the number her sire had.

"Daniel?" Constance whispered. "Who is he? What does he want?"

Daniel gave some kind of signal to Maggie, then answered her question. "'Tis Blair Lamont, and my guess is he wants you."

CHAPTER TWENTY-FIVE

IF CONSTANCE COULD MELD HER body any tighter to Daniel's, she'd probably knock him off his horse. No matter—she inched even closer. "I may have to send you into the kirk," he whispered to her.

"Nay! He'll grab me. Please, Daniel. I want to stay with you."

Lamont finally answered Maggie. "I'm not interested in passing. In fact, we have joined with that man over there—" he gestured to the right, "—to make our requests. We've made a deal, the two of us. That way, we've enough men to fight you for what we want. We aren't afraid of Lockhart's men. They're Lowlanders."

"And what is it you want?" Will asked as he lifted his arm to call his falcons down closer to the group, their swooping unsettling some of Lamont's men.

"We want two things. Give me that heart-shaped gem, and my friend will take the girl. If you cooperate, we will leave you without raising a sword."

Constance gasped.

"Daughter, give it to him," her sire said. "Your life is worth far more than that silly stone."

To her surprise, she could see worry in her sire's face. The façade of the stone-cold warrior began to crack, showing glints of the caring sire she remembered from childhood. Had the mother abbess been right? Had his threats all been for show?

He'd ordered her to give her beloved mother's stone away, but she wouldn't do it. She'd keep it safe and return it to her dear mother when she had the chance.

Constance patted her gown, searching for the feel of it inside the pocket, but she couldn't find it. She whispered to Daniel, "'Tis not there."

"Lass, you gathered your things in haste. I've no doubt 'tis there, but you'll not give it to that bastard."

Lamont searched Daniel's face. "Nice to see you again, Damien. Or is that your real name? I should have known you were involved with the Grant bastards. My gut told me not to trust you." He snickered as he stared at Constance and Daniel. "You do have taste. She's a bonny one. Lass, give me the stone and I'll take my men away, and I promise not to hurt your friend there. If you don't give it to me, I'll kill you both and then search you for it."

A loud voice interrupted him. "Like hell you will. You promised to stay and fight with me," the leader of the group to their right barked.

"Who is that?" Constance whispered.

"I don't know," Daniel said. "I've not seen the man before." He then asked the question they were all thinking. "What do you want with the lass? Who pays you?"

"Jean MacDole pays me. And she pays me well. Now hand over the girl or I'll kill you."

Constance gasped again. "Why does that cruel woman want me? Poor Rose. What a mean-spirited person her mother is." She had no idea how Jean MacDole was able to give orders to anyone. The cruel woman had admitted to two murders, and everyone had seemed to believe she was headed to prison.

"I don't know, lass, but we've plenty of other troubles just now," Daniel whispered, rubbing her arm. He turned his horse around so they faced the intruders, their backs now to her sire.

"Gil, when you get her, you'll hand over that stone as we

agreed," Lamont said to the man across from him. Now the two fools were acting as if the rest of them weren't even there.

"Aye, we did, until you decided to back out of your part. Mayhap I'll keep the stone for myself." Gil looked quite pleased with himself, while his men snickered behind him.

Maggie glanced at Constance and nodded her head, indicating the time had come for her to take the stone out of her pocket. Speaking only loud enough for Constance and Daniel to hear, she said, "Pull it out of your pocket and show it to all. 'Twill buy us time."

"And then you must dismount," Daniel said. "I want you in the kirk. This will turn into a battle."

Constance climbed down with Daniel's help, and her sire called out, "Good girl. Now walk straight over to me and I'll take you home."

She ignored her sire and searched her pocket again, all the while making her way toward the church. If she were close enough to run inside, she would be safe. She glanced up at Maggie and then shifted her gaze to Daniel before she announced, "I can't find it. I must have lost it."

Her sire groaned, but Lamont and Gil both shouted in unison, "Liar!"

Lamont, the fury in his face growing, shouted, "You have one minute to find it and then I'll cut your hand off, strip you, and find it myself."

Out of nowhere came another group of riders. Daniel had no idea how they had crept up on the group so quietly, though the multitude of men and riders gathered around the kirk did make quite a din and the night was dark enough to provide some cover.

"You touch that lass and you're a dead man." Logan Ramsay's voice rang out over the land. Daniel's father rode beside Uncle Logan, and dozens of Ramsay and Drummond guards were gathered behind them.

Daniel noticed his brother, David, behind his sire. Apparently, his brother had gone home to bring more men to assist him. He couldn't help but smile at this unexpected development. He motioned for Constance to continue toward the kirk, and Maggie, still on horseback, rode beside her as protection. His cousin was an expert with the bow, and he had no doubt she'd find a hiding place where she could use her weapon once Constance was safely inside.

As Will moved over to join the Ramsay group, Daniel took a moment to assess his surroundings. Lamont was now in front of him, and his sire and uncle had taken up a position directly to his right. On their right, the Band of Cousins had emerged and stood ready to fight, then Constance's sire was next in the circle, followed by Gil, who had come at the request of Jean MacDole, the witch who'd tried to sell her own daughter to the Channel of Dubh.

Constance looked so tiny against all those warriors and the horses. She was almost into the kirk, so he maneuvered his horse to put him in a position to fight Gil first. His sire's group could easily handle Lamont. At this point, he was hoping Constance's sire would order his guards to take up arms after Gil's men.

War whoops echoed into the night, and the place erupted into a full battlefield. Gil and his men charged toward Daniel, forcing him to look away from Constance.

He swung his sword, using his left forearm as support while he controlled his horse with his knees, something they'd practiced over and over again in the lists. He took Gil out with two swings, then knocked the next two off their horses with one wide swipe of his blade.

Arrows sluiced through the air around him, finding their targets as he knew they would. Gavin and Gregor had learned from Aunt Gwyneth, who never missed her mark. He had a quick moment to assess the area before he was swept up in the next wave of the attack.

The Ramsay and Drummond warriors were making easy work of Lamont's men, though he did not see Blair

Lamont on horseback or among the fallen men. Just as he'd hoped, Lockhart's men had joined his cousins in attacking Gil's men, so their numbers were dwindling quickly.

One warrior came straight at him, his arms raised overhead to deliver a killing blow, but Daniel caught him square in his belly before he could manage it. The next fighter bellowed but barely lifted his sword before Daniel caught him in his side, forcing him off his horse.

Men came at him and at him, an endless number of fighters and beasts until he thought he could stand it no more. "Constance. Where is Constance?" he shouted, desperate to know if she'd made it to safety.

Connor yelled, "Lamont just grabbed her." He drew up alongside Daniel and said, "Go. I'll take care of these fools."

Connor could swing a sword faster than anyone he knew, so he gladly turned around and rode hard to the back of the church. Maggie pointed off in the distance as she mounted her own horse.

Constance was on horseback with Blair Lamont.

What the hell was he to do?

He flicked the reins and flew after Lamont, setting a frantic pace. His horse loved competition nearly as much as he did.

With a certainty he'd never before possessed, he knew one thing.

Blair Lamont was a dead man.

CHAPTER TWENTY-SIX

———————

D ANIEL CHASED LAMONT UNTIL HE thought he would be forced to give up. His horse was panting and losing steam, and Lamont's was racing forward as if a fire had been lit beneath him, but someone must have been looking out for them, because Lamont's horse took a tumble just before it leaped over a burn. Daniel got close enough to reach for Lamont. He grabbed his tunic with his *Treun* and tugged him clear off the horse. To his surprise, the appendage flew off, landing far away from him.

He didn't care. He had to save Constance, with or without *Treun*.

The bastard fell to the ground with a grunt. Constance screamed, rolling off the horse as Lamont fought to gain his feet again. She hadn't fallen far, so Daniel focused on Lamont, who had already found his feet.

The man drew his sword and shot straight at Daniel, who had jumped down from his horse to fight him. Blair had to be upset because he was swinging wildly, like a lad who'd just learned how to hold a sword.

Daniel parried with the man until Lamont was heavily fatigued.

Then, because he would just as soon bring the man in alive so they could question him about the Channel of Dubh, he said, "Drop your sword and I'll allow you to live."

Blair did drop his sword, but then he attempted the stupidest thing possible. He pulled out a small dagger and reached for Constance. Daniel's strong wife scratched and kicked like the fighter he knew her to be. Daniel dropped his weapon and charged toward them, intent on pushing her away from the man so he could finish him, but he slipped and caught Lamont's dagger in his thigh.

Daniel roared like a wolf on a mountaintop. He grabbed the bastard by the throat, choking him, but he lost his grip. Lamont stood up and stepped back, then immediately turned and lunged for Constance. Fear and rage painted Daniel's vision. He was too far from his sword, so he pulled out his dagger and plunged it straight into Lamont's heart. The bastard gasped, staring at him, then tried to clutch his arm before he crumpled to the ground, dead.

Daniel reached for Constance, but his leg gave out. She was at his side, holding him, trembling, kissing him furiously. "Daniel, Daniel, I was so afraid." His hand came up to touch her cheek, and it was covered in blood. His blood.

He just stared at it, his eyes blurring a bit. He settled on the ground, confused, wondering why he could no longer stand up.

"Daniel, oh my…Daniel…" She stared at his leg, her eyes wide with horror, then reached inside her pocket for something. "I found it. I couldn't find it before, but now I have. Here, this is supposed to be magical for wounds."

"What?" Daniel couldn't make any sense of her words, but he grasped her upper arm, grateful he'd managed to save her from Lamont. He hadn't needed *Treun* to protect her, after all. "Now we can marry. I love you, Constance."

"Oh, Daniel. There's too much blood. Oh, what shall I do?" She fell to her knees and placed the gemstone against his wound, trying to wipe the blood away with her gown. "Please Daniel, please don't die. I couldn't bear it."

There was a tree not far from them, and Connor appeared from behind it. He dropped from his horse to assist her, followed by Maggie.

Daniel caught the shock in Connor's eyes, and knew he

was in bad shape from that look alone. Maggie was a bit better at hiding her concern, but she immediately jumped into action. "We need to stem his bleeding."

"Connor, help me up. I'll be fine," Daniel said, the expressions on everyone's faces scaring the hell out of him.

"Nay, you'll not get up, Daniel. You'll stay there until we stem the bleeding, then you're going straight to a healer. We'll see which one your sire recommends.

Daniel couldn't understand all of Maggie's words, as if some came to him and others didn't. His eyes drifted closed only to jerk open at another sound. "It hurt really bad, but now…"

Maggie said, "We need to keep him awake. Daniel, stay with us."

Daniel's gaze caught Maggie's again, but he couldn't recall what she'd just said. "I wish to marry Constance right away."

"You will as soon as we stop the bleeding, Daniel. You have to be able to stand next to your bride, do you not?" Maggie whispered, her voice falling off at the end as if she were choking something back.

His eyes drifted shut again, but another bellow awakened him.

Maggie screamed, "Papa?"

He glanced at the panicked expression on his cousin's face. When had he last seen her look this concerned? And why was Maggie calling him Papa? He'd ask her as soon as he closed his eyes for just a wee bit longer.

"Help me, Connor," Constance said, eager. They moved him over to the tree so he could lean against it, but Daniel would not let go of his wee, fierce wife.

"Don't leave me, Constance. Promise me." His hand still gripped her arm.

"I promise, Daniel, if you promise not to die on me."

CONSTANCE WAS SUDDENLY POSSESSED BY a need that consumed her. Gavin, Gregor, and Braden had joined them, so she turned to the Band of Cousins and said, "Braden, go find the priest. I wish to marry Daniel right now."

Daniel smiled at her and whispered, "Good idea. I love you." His eyes closed and she became frantic, fearful that he would not wake up.

Connor handed her a linen he'd found somewhere. "Here, Constance. Use this on his leg."

"This is too small to soak up the blood," she said, hating how her voice shook. She needed to be strong. "What do I do with it?"

"Push on it," Connor said. "Here, allow me. I'll get it to stop bleeding."

Constance leaned down and kissed Daniel. 'Please wake up, my love. I need you to wake up. You must be able to agree to our marriage."

She glanced at Maggie and said, "Here, hold this gemstone over the wound. 'Tis said it holds magical properties for healing."

Maggie nodded and settled the stone near the wound on his leg, the blood now slowing a bit from Connor's compression.

Cheers echoed behind them. "What is it?" Constance asked, just then noticing Daniel's sire and uncle were coming toward them, David not far behind.

Will said, "We've ended the battle. Gil's men and Lamont's men are either dead or they've run off."

Daniel's uncle glanced past them to Lamont's slumped body on the ground. "Well done, Daniel, I assume," he said with a jolly tone. "Lamont will not be causing us any more trouble."

"Papa," Maggie said, her tone dropped. "We need a healer for Daniel."

Micheil Ramsay joined in the well wishes until his gaze

fell on his son, laid back against the tree. "Hellfire. Here, lass," he said, as he hurried to his son's side. "I'll move him into the kirk."

"I'll help you," Logan said. "We'll get him inside and send for the Drummond healer."

Then the others all started voicing their opinions at once, confusing her too much for her to respond.

"Nay, send for Aunt Jennie," someone insisted.

"Leave him here until we stop the bleeding," said Connor.

Will said, "I can try some salve I have."

Maggie said, "The priest is almost here, Constance."

The voices started to bleed into one another, so much so she could no longer identify who'd spoken. She slumped over, barely heeding what was said.

"He's probably going to die with all that blood."

"It doesn't look good for Daniel."

"Why the hell were they out here?"

"All that fighting and Daniel's going to die…"

"Get him off the ground."

"Get him to the church."

"We need to get him to a healer."

"Constance," her sire called out to her from a short distance away, his voice standing out from the others. "Come away from there."

Constance had heard enough. With a frenzy she hadn't know she ever possessed, she stood and screamed, "Back away! All of you! Back. Away. And stop giving me advice. I want you all a hundred paces away from us except for Connor and Maggie, who know what they're to do."

Some began to move, others smirked, while her sire said, "Do not talk to me that way." His eyes had that fearsome look they got whenever she dared stand up to him. But she would not be swayed now. Not when Daniel's life was endangered.

"He's my nephew," Logan said, not standing down either.

"Back away, lass, and we'll take care of him."

Micheil's hand moved to Logan's arm and squeezed.

Constance reached into her boot and yanked her dagger out. "Back away, I say. Now I'll tell all of you how this will go. This is my husband. We are married, but we want—" She paused for a brief moment just to choke back her tears. "We want the priest's blessing on our marriage, and that is going to happen…before anything else does." She tried but failed to stop the hitch in her voice every time she gazed at her dear Daniel.

"Constance. I'll not tell you again. Come here!" Her sire's booming voice carried over everyone else's.

She whirled around in a fury. "You will not order me about again, Papa. Aye, you're my sire, but this is my husband, and I will do what I need to in order to save his life."

Silence fell over the group as Constance swiped at the tears on her face and walked around the periphery of the clearing, making sure everyone stood back, her dagger still held in her hand. Her gown, still drenched in blood, was hardly the right thing for her to marry in, but she didn't care. She stopped in front of Micheil Ramsay and said, "Forgive me. I know he's your son, but he's my husband, and I will do what I believe is right."

She may have imagined it, but she thought she saw a spark of admiration in Micheil Ramsay's eyes.

Maggie said, "What else can we do, Constance?"

"Please send for a healer. Whose land is closest?"

Logan Ramsay said, "Already done, lass. The Drummond healer will be at their keep soon, and my sister-in-law will arrive in another two hours. She's the best in all of Scotland. But first we must get him to Drummond land. 'Tis a short distance from here."

The priest came up behind Micheil Ramsay but immediately stepped back once he saw the dagger in Constance's hand.

She didn't miss the shock in his gaze. She brushed the

hair back from her face and said, "Father, there's a marriage we need you for. I'll put this away if everyone agrees to stand back."

She strode over to her sire, who said to her in a much lower voice this time, "I'm only trying to keep you from being hurt, daughter. Aye, I am hard on you, but you are still my lass."

"'Tis too late for that, Papa. I'm a woman, and I'm married. I will make my own decisions now and in the future."

Her father surprised her by dismounting and striding over to stand in front of her. Afraid he would try to force her to leave, she kept her distance. She sheathed her dagger but kept her hand poised to grab it again, if necessary. Though she doubted she could bring herself to use it against her sire, she would threaten him if need be.

"This isnae what I wanted for you or any of my children. 'Tis wrong to be in the midst of all this Highland chaos. I promise to find you a good husband. Come home, we all miss you."

His tone shocked her as much as his words. He'd missed her, too. She'd not expected that. And yet, there could be only one answer.

"'Tis too late. I love my husband. I hope you will approve of our marriage someday, but even if you don't, I will stay by his side. As soon as he is healed, I promise to return the stone, but we're in desperate need of it now. Tell Mama I'm sorry."

Her sire nodded, moving back toward his horse, but stopped before he mounted. "Lass, you're stronger than I would have believed. We all love you." He tipped his head to her before he mounted, his features turning fierce and determined once again, and turned his horse around. All she could do was watch as he and his men galloped off into the distance.

She would not cry over her father, even if he had acknowledged she was strong.

She would *not*. She would prove the truth of his words by keeping herself together.

The priest appeared at her side while Daniel's brother David spoke to his cousins off to the side. She didn't care what they did as long as they didn't interfere with their wedding. Connor and Maggie had stayed with Daniel, still seeing to his wounds.

"Father, we're ready." Maggie's voice was strong, just as she wished her own would be.

Constance moved back to Daniel's side and kissed him. "My love, the priest is here. He will marry us now." She couldn't stop the tears any longer, allowing them to roll down her cheeks unchecked.

His beautiful forest green eyes fluttered open, and he smiled at her. "We're getting married? Naught would please me more."

The priest moved over to stand in front of them. David approached the tree with the rest of the cousins. He leaned down to speak with Connor, who then lifted the fabric he held over Daniel's wound, peering at the blood. "I think 'tis slowed enough."

Maggie returned the stone to Constance, who placed it in her pocket, then went over to join Will.

"We're ready, Father," Constance said at once.

David said, "Give us a moment, Constance. Please?"

She nearly smirked at him. She supposed she had acted like a daft person, but it was what she had needed to do to get them all to listen to her.

Constance stood back while the cousins collectively gathered around Daniel, maneuvered something underneath him, then lifted him into the air. They'd placed two plaids under him, and the cousins all stood at the edges, ready to hold him up for the ceremony.

Daniel's eyes flew open and he looked around in shock, but then his expression quickly changed to a wide smile. Maggie ran back into the clearing and handed Constance a bouquet of flowers she'd just picked from the forest.

Constance could have cried over both gestures, but she forced herself to stand strong. "Go ahead, Father."

Daniel managed to stay awake during most of the ceremony, though his eyes did close on two occasions. Gavin, the jokester, managed to pinch him back awake until they all laughed.

And oh, how wonderful it was to hear her Daniel's laugh. "I love you, my sweet," he said, "and this is the best wedding I could have ever asked for." His gaze took in all his loved ones surrounding them.

David muttered, "Mama will kill you, but she'll love Constance enough to keep you alive. It'll help your case that you're hurt."

The priest continued, and they said their vows, the priest finally blessing them as husband and wife to the cheers of all those in attendance. Daniel kissed her and the crowd cheered again, but then a cart came into their vision, and Micheil said, "Lass. We've allowed the wedding. You're husband and wife officially, but 'tis time to get Daniel to a healer."

Constance nodded to him and said, "I'll be there all along the way, Daniel. And my thanks to all who allowed me to have my way."

Gavin snorted. "I'll never cross you. I'd run through a pack of snapping wolves first."

"Nor will I," Logan said, although he had none of the bluster she'd seen in him before. "Lass, you remind me of my wife. I'll keep my distance whenever your temper riles."

Micheil leaned over and kissed her cheek. "Welcome to Clan Ramsay and Clan Drummond, Constance. We're proud to call you family."

CHAPTER TWENTY- SEVEN

CONSTANCE RODE IN THE CART with Daniel's head cradled on her lap. They'd positioned him so she could continue to press on the wound to staunch the bleeding. He slept most of the ride, which made her extremely anxious, but she didn't think he'd had much sleep lately. Mayhap he simply had some catching up to do.

She only realized they'd reached Drummond land when a beautiful woman rode her horse up next to the cart, continuing on abreast of them. "How is my son, and who are you?"

Daniel opened his eyes at the sound of his mother's voice. "Mama, greetings to you. Meet my wife, Constance Lockhart of Lee. I seem to have gotten myself into a mess again. Do not blame Constance." His head fell back into Constance's lap.

Diana Drummond's wide-eyed gaze took in all the blood, then shifted to Constance's face. "You are his wife? What happened?"

Before she could reply, Micheil Ramsay rode up on the other side of Diana's horse. He filled her in on the details, speaking in a hushed voice.

Constance took the opportunity to assess the woman. Diana's hair was the shade of the midnight sky with strands of red and silver here and there. She understood where Daniel's good looks came from, though Micheil Ramsay was still a fine-looking man.

Diana sat her horse as well as any gifted equestrian. Had she ever crossed the path of a more beautiful and regal looking woman? She thought not.

Diana was gorgeous, talented, smart, and the laird of her clan.

She would probably hate Constance.

But Constance wouldn't worry about that just yet. Her focus had to be on Daniel.

"Diana," someone bellowed. She thought she recognized Logan Ramsay's distinctive voice. "You'll not want to cross her. She reminds me of my Gwynie."

Diana turned back toward Constance. The only emotion she could read on the laird's face was concern. "We have the Drummond healer in the hall awaiting his arrival. His aunts will both be arriving soon. They are the best healers in the Highlands. How much has he been sleeping?"

No other sound could be heard but the trampling of the horses' hooves across the meadow and Constance's own sniffling. "He's having a difficult time staying awake. I've tried, but he's so fatigued. He's lost much blood."

"More than what you have on your gown?"

Constance peered down at her gown again and finally nodded, unable to speak the words.

Diana paused for a moment, then said, "Welcome to Clan Drummond, daughter. If Daniel loves you, I'm certain I will. Do you love my son?"

"More than I ever thought possible."

The majestic woman smiled. "Then he will fight to live. I know him verra well."

How she prayed Diana was right.

———◆———

DANIEL WAS RUNNING THROUGH THE meadow, chasing after Constance. She giggled and glanced over her shoulder at him.

"Come, you must catch me. 'Tis the only way!"

He chuckled and played the game, but then he stepped on something that gave him a sharp pain, one that carried all the way up his leg. Something had bitten him. He swung at the beast as it tried to bite him again, but he had no hand. In fact, he'd somehow lost both hands. When he looked down, his leg was disappearing, piece by piece, though the critter had run off.

Where was his leg going?

And what had happened to his other hand?

Constance turned around and looked at him, a sad expression on her face. "I'm so sorry, Daniel. I cannot spend my life with a man with no hands and one leg. Goodbye!"

"Constance, wait! I love you! Don't leave me, please! Constance!"

Something pulled him back and he awoke with a start. "Daniel, hush. 'Tis all right. You're having a bad dream. Your aunties will save you."

"Constance?" He gripped her hand with his one hand, relieved that he at least had that, then released her to shove the covers away. "My leg. What has happened?"

"Daniel, calm down. Here. Drink this." Her hand touched his cheek and she turned him to face her.

"Constance. Please don't leave me. I want to marry you."

"We *are* married. You're confused from the fever." She held the cup to his lips and he drank, the water soothing his dry throat. What had happened?

Her calm voice continued to explain. "We were in a battle and you saved me, but the man managed to cut your leg. It wasn't a large cut, but 'twas deep. There was too much blood, but you're healing now. Do not worry. I will take care of you. Daniel, don't you remember that we married at the kirk? We said our vows and I promised never to leave you. You're my husband and I love you."

He stared up at Constance, his eyes finally managing to catch her gaze. She offered him more water and he drank as much as he could. "Aunt Brenna. I must speak with her," he whispered.

Footsteps approached the side of his bed. "What is it, Daniel? I'm here. Aunt Jennie is with me. We've taken care of your leg. 'Tis still oozing so it may pain you a great deal. I can give you more potion."

"Nay, please. No more. I need to understand what is happening. And what do you mean you've taken care of my leg? Did you cut it off, Aunt Brenna?" The horror of the dream still thrummed in his blood. His hand reached down in search of his appendage, but it was the opposite leg and difficult to reach just now.

"Nay, nay," Aunt Brenna said. "We've been tending the discharge, but 'tis finally slowing. Daniel, you seem upset. What is it?"

"Do you recall what I told you the day after I lost my hand?"

"Aye. I recall it verra well. Why do you speak of it now?"

"Because I've changed my mind."

"About what?" Constance asked.

He turned his face back to look at his dear wife. "A couple of days after I lost my hand, it hurt so much that I told Aunt Brenna I would have rather died than to go on without it."

"Oh, Daniel," Constance whispered, kissing his forehead.

His mother came up behind Aunt Brenna. "I remember, Daniel. I was there. What say you now?"

Daniel stared at Constance before he turned back to his mother and his aunt. "I feel completely different. If you must take my leg, then do it. I'd rather lose it in order to live by my wife's side."

———

CONSTANCE HAD FALLEN ASLEEP NEXT to Daniel. His fever had finally dropped. His aunts had been fastidious about applying the salve on his wound. They'd washed the green discharge away many times before it finally stopped coming. Perhaps today would be the day he would awaken and speak with her.

Aunt Brenna had promised her that he was on the mend. The rest was up to him.

A light knock sounded at the door. "Enter," she said, shuffling out from beneath the covers to find a robe to don. His dear mother had supplied her with almost everything she could have ever wanted, including clean gowns and night rails.

Now if she could only restore her husband to health.

Diana stuck her head around the door and said, "You have visitors. They're in the great hall. If you're too tired to speak with them tonight, I can find them a chamber to rest in for the night. 'Tis nearly midnight."

"Visitors? Who is it?" she asked, perplexed.

"Your mother and your sister Denise. Shall I lead them to their chamber for the night or would you like to speak with them now?"

Constance was stunned. She'd feared she'd never see her mother and sister again. "My sire? Is he here to take me away?"

Diana shook her head. "He's here, but he'll not take you away, lass. I told him he'd have to kill a hundred of our men to take you from us. He convinced me that he just wishes to see that you're hale. He told me you made him proud that day on the battlefield." She strode over to stand in front of her, fussing with Constance's hair to make her more presentable. "I wish I'd been there to see you fight for my son. Daniel won't let you go, and neither will I. We've become quite fond of you. I see why my son has fallen in love with you. 'Tis clear to me that he's fought this battle with the fever for you."

Constance hugged Diana and mumbled, "My thanks," through her tears. "I'll see them now."

"Go," Diana said softly. "Go, and I'll sit with my son. And

Constance?"

"Aye, my lady?" She stopped before she searched out something for her feet.

"I'll do whatever you like. They are welcome to stay a few days, or I'll send them out. You let me know your preference."

Constance found her slippers and stepped into the passageway, pausing a moment to allow her eyes to adjust to the bright torches. The Drummond keep was quite majestic. Every detail had been carefully tended to. She couldn't wait until Daniel was hale enough to show her around the castle, especially the gardens because she'd heard so much about them. It was only a bit larger than Lee Castle, but it was much more regal, with curved woodwork and beautiful tapestries set against dark wood. The bed chambers had a new type of woven covering on the floors that was lovely to walk on.

Lee Castle was kept clean because her dear mother insisted on it, but the chambers were all filled by her brothers and sisters. In fact, the lads had always shared one chamber and the lassies another, because space was limited. They had no room for overnight guests. The few times they'd had guests, the lads had been forced to sleep in the hall. But her mother had worked hard to make their home cozy, and indeed it was. She still missed the fragrance of pine in the great hall from the garlands and baskets full of greenery her mother often used as decorations.

They were all part of her past.

She took a deep breath and headed to the stairs, overjoyed to see her dearest sister standing at the base.

"Constance? 'Tis truly you?"

"Oh, Denise, I've missed you so." She hurried down the stairs and threw herself at her sister, wrapping her arms around her with a glee she'd not felt in a long time. Her mother appeared behind her sister, tears in her eyes.

"Daughter, I feared we'd never see you again." Tears slid

down her cheeks. Her mother did nothing to chase them away, instead staring at Constance with a look she didn't understand. "You've grown into a woman, lass."

She stepped away from her sister and embraced her mother. "Mama, I'm so sorry for everything. I wanted to tell you, but…"

Her mother stepped back and shushed her. "Never mind. I just need to take you in, convince myself that naught is wrong with you." Her fingers moved up to brush a tear away from her cheek. "You've had a challenging time, so Lady Drummond has said."

"Mama, I'm fine. I'm married. I love my husband, but he was hurt in a battle. But what about Papa? Diana told me he came with you."

The door from the outside opened and her sire stood on the threshold. She'd expected him to shout at her, or simply give her a withering look, but she couldn't read the expression on his face. Micheil Ramsay was behind him. He ushered them over to the cushioned chairs in front of the hearth.

"We've plenty of ale. I'm sure I can find a small repast. Sit down. Talk with your daughter, but I'll tell you, Douglas, you'll not be taking that lass away from us. We're all quite fond of her." He smiled and headed toward the kitchen to find a serving lass.

Constance sat in a chair in the middle and folded her hands in her lap, awaiting the inevitable chastisement from her sire. But something had changed inside her.

She no longer feared the man.

True, he was her sire and she would always respect him. She had many fond memories of her childhood with both of her parents. Her sire could be harsh, but he'd always treated his family with love—until the day he forsook her. What would he say to her now? Had he truly forgiven her?

She lifted her gaze to his and waited.

"Och, lass, my apologies to you. I know we've had some difficult times. I told you 'twas all about the necklace, but 'twas a lie. I chased you because your mother and siblings would not let up until I found you." He took a deep breath and sat down opposite her. "I missed you, too, and we were all worried. We had no idea where you went. Why did you run away, lass? We could have worked this out."

Her mother coughed and glared at her father. Denise slid her chair closer to Constance's and reached for her hand to give her support. She squeezed her sister's hand in return to let her know how much she had missed her.

"Papa, that day we met in the solar, you made so many threats, I did not know what to believe. Lashings, islands, sending Denise away. I did not know what to think or do next. I know I made a mistake, but I didn't wish to live alone forever on an island, nor did I wish to be whipped in front of all *or* tied to a post. And I could not bear the thought of Denise suffering for my mistake."

Her sister gasped and covered her mouth with her hand. "Papa!" Denise apparently hadn't heard the full story.

She patted her sister's hand. "Do not fash yourself, sister. I'm verra happy now." Tears brimmed in her eyes. Her sire opened his mouth to say something, but she held her hand up. "Papa, I'll tell you the same. I'm verra happy where I am. I love Daniel and I wish to stay here."

She glanced at her mother, who was looking at her with such a look of pride that it humbled her.

"Constance, I was angry," her sire said, "and my wee temper got the best of me."

"Wee temper?" her mother sputtered.

"I was verra upset. It does not often happen that I travel to the village stables and hear snipes gossiping about my sweet daughter. I wanted to grab him by the neck and choke him until his eyes popped out of his head."

"Papa, I made a mistake, but I was also naïve. He used trickery on me."

"I understand that now. The bastard finally came to the keep and confessed that he'd tricked you into it. His sire had him by the neck, or he never would have admitted it. I'm glad to see you are not carrying, but I cannot believe you truly thought I would leave you on a deserted island."

"'Tis what you threatened, among other things," she leaned toward him, her own anger building inside her. How could he have made such a threat if had no intention of carrying it out? What was she to think? He had never been the sort to make empty threats.

"I know what I said, but I was trying to scare you. And I wished to scare Denise too, so she'd not be so foolish."

"But I heard you tell our steward to ready the boat. I had no choice but to run away."

"I was only taunting you. I never would have done it." He pointed to her mother. "She would have sliced me into pieces and thrown me to the wolves if I ever tried to do such a thing."

Her mother chuckled, something she didn't often hear. She had a look of profound relief.

Rising from his chair, her sire came to stand in front of her. After a moment, he reached for her hand and pulled her to standing. The gesture put a knot in her throat. Back home, he used to lecture her from on high, while she sat in a chair, but he had just lifted her to his level, or near enough given the difference in their heights.

"I made a mistake," he said. "and for that I apologize. I also must say that while you nearly scared every hair on my head into the wind, you did make me proud, and I think you've wed a fine man. I could not have chosen better for you. I've asked many of my acquaintances about your husband, and everything I've heard indicates he's a man worthy of our pride. His sire and mother are also fine people."

"Truly, Papa?"

"Truly." He kissed the top of her head and she fell into

her sire's arms.

"You frightened me, Papa."

"You've matured in a verra short time, lassie. Forgive me?"

"Aye, you're forgiven, Papa. As long as you never threaten Denise."

Her father chuckled. "I won't. But you did surprise me. You've given me the honor of being able to brag about how my daughter held Logan and Micheil Ramsay back with naught but a threat and her dagger."

Micheil returned with several goblets of ale and a hunk of cheese and three apples. "'Tis the best I can do at this hour. My wife is at Daniel's side."

"You'll stay a few days?" Constance asked. "I'd like you all to meet Daniel."

"Or course, we will. I cannot wait to hear all about your adventures. I hear you've had quite a few," her mother said, gratefully accepting the goblet.

Denise stood and hugged her again. "You must tell me everything," she said, pulling back to look at her with glittering eyes. "You've done things none of us have. Running away, being kidnapped, and taking part in a battle…and now you're married! 'Tis most exciting, Constance!"

Constance hugged her sister back. "I'm so happy to see you, but it has been trying. If you don't mind, let's save the tale for another day. I'm tired, and I'd like to go back to my husband."

Micheil said to her family, "Diana will be back momentarily. Once you finish your repast, she'll show you to your chambers."

"'Tis not inconvenient?" her mother asked, standing next to Constance.

"Nay, we're happy to have you join us for a few days. We have plenty of room for you, and I'm sure your daughter has much to share with you. I'd also be happy to have you meet our son, Daniel. He is a fine man and we are quite proud of him."

Constance turned to leave, but her mother stopped her with a hand on her arm.

"Just one question before you go, my dear. Your sister and I are most curious about something."

Denise nodded and whispered, "Please?"

"What is it?" Constance asked, stopping to turn back to them.

"Where did you go when you first left? We searched everywhere for you."

"To Sona Abbey in the Highlands."

Her parents' eyes widened.

"All the way to the Highlands by yourself?" her sire whispered. "You're more resilient than I thought."

She lifted her chin a notch. "I ran into a family going to visit their daughter there. They were kind to me and invited me to travel with them. I was going to take my vows and become a nun."

Her sister choked.

CHAPTER TWENTY-EIGHT

———◆———

CONSTANCE CLIMBED INTO BED, WEARY but satisfied. Her sire didn't hate her. Her mother and sister had been overjoyed to see her. And, most importantly, Daniel was healing and she'd been accepted by his clan. It was hard to believe it had been nearly a sennight since they'd married, but much of their days had been spent fighting his fever.

Daniel had won his battle, with Blair Lamont and his wound. While he slept often, he'd finally awakened enough to eat and get out of bed, though he hadn't yet traveled down the stairs. Still weak, he hadn't even attempted to leave their chamber. He slept on his side, his breathing telling her the fever had indeed dissipated. She'd bathed him earlier, and she'd been grateful his parents had not been in the chamber as his randiness had caused her to blush, but she'd refused him. She was a wee bit randy herself, in truth, but she feared getting caught.

She turned on her side and backed up to his front, hoping to absorb some of his heat. Sleeping next to him was nearly the same as sleeping next to a hearth, even when he didn't have a fever. She missed his arm around her, but she didn't wish to awaken him.

Some time later, she was nearly asleep when his arm wrapped around her and tugged her back against him—only for her to brush up against something distinctly hard and hot.

And distinctly Daniel.

She heard a husky groan as his hand fell to her bottom before it snaked around to her front, finding one of her breasts without the need of any guidance.

"Daniel?"

"Hmmm?"

He continued to caress her breast until she could feel her body thrum from his soft touch, his thumb brushing her nipple until she moaned. Horrified, she clapped her own hand over her mouth. She couldn't let anyone else hear her or she'd be mortified.

His breath warmed her neck. "I just couldn't recall how beautiful you are, so since 'tis still dark, I have to feel my way to your beauty. Nay, you know that's a lie. I could never forget how beautiful you are. Are you well?"

"Aye, even better now," she whispered. It struck her that her parents were in the great hall with his parents. Mayhap this was a good time. Who knew when they'd have their next opportunity to be together.

"Oh, Daniel, that feels so good." She could feel his warm breath on her shoulder as he expertly kissed and nibbled her skin. She tipped her head to give him better access to her neck, but then his hand moved down to the vee between her legs. As soon as he touched the right spot, her legs parted to give him better access. She moaned as he thrust a finger into her.

He chuckled softly, a sweet sound. "You're as randy as I am, lass."

She rolled onto her back and gazed up at him as he continued to tease her, stroking her until she was ready to beg for more, but there was a slight problem. "Daniel, I want you, but how can we do this? Your leg will pain you, and I don't wish to answer to your aunts if you tear any of your stitches. What can we do?" Her breathing had already turned into frantic pants because she needed him inside her. "Daniel, please?"

He ravished her mouth, showing her with his tongue exactly what he wished to do to her elsewhere, stoking her until she was in a frenzy. Then he abruptly stopped, rolled onto his back, and said, "Get on top of me."

She stared at him, confused as to what exactly he wanted her to do.

His breathing was as frenzied as her own as he took her hand and settled it on his shaft. "Guide me inside you."

He was so hot and hard that the feel of him sent her closer to the edge. Stroking him up and down with her hand, she managed to lift one leg over him until she straddled him.

"Now, lass. Take me inside." His hand gripped her hip and guided her, helping her approach him from the right angle.

"Now what?"

"Lift up and guide me in."

Hell, but she needed him inside her so badly that she did what he asked. She found she quite liked the tease of his tip at her entrance so she played with that a bit until she got him exactly where she wanted him. A moan escaped her as she seated herself completely on him, and he set a quick pace that sent her careening into a climax. He grasped her hip and surged inside of her until they were both spent.

She collapsed to the side of him with the silliest grin she'd ever worn, she was certain of it.

———◆———

THREE DAYS LATER, THE FAMILY was happily settled in the Drummond great hall. Constance's mother, sister, and sire had all gone home. Daniel had enjoyed meeting them, especially Denise, who reminded him so much of Constance.

He knew it had troubled Constance to disappoint her parents, but the heart-shaped red gemstone had not turned up anywhere. She remembered using it on Daniel's wound and placing it in her pocket, but it must have fallen out somewhere between the kirk and the keep.

No one had found it. Or if someone had, they hadn't reported it.

Constance had cried and apologized profusely to her mother, explaining that she'd only taken the necklace so she had something to remember her mother by.

Her mother hadn't seemed to be bothered by it at all. "I have you back. 'Tis all that matters."

They took their leave, and Constance and Daniel promised to visit the barony in another moon or two.

Daniel's leg had improved greatly. Though the wound was not overly large, he'd still felt weak for a few days. Even so, he'd tried to convince the others he could get out of bed and go to the lists with his new hand, but Aunt Brenna had taken to hanging Constance's blood-drenched gown over the window to remind him why he couldn't go.

The family was gathered by the hearth, each with a goblet in hand, when the door banged open with the same memorable force the lads had heard many times over the years.

"Greetings, Logan," Micheil said, without turning to see who'd arrived. "Someday I'm quite certain the door will fall off thanks to your delicate ways." He couldn't help but grin at his brother. Daniel knew how much his sire loved Uncle Logan, and how proud he was of the work Logan and Gwyneth did for the Scottish Crown.

Aunt Gwyneth came in behind him, shaking her head at her husband's brash entrance. Daniel's mother and father both liked to say that she was still as lithe and striking as the day they'd first met her at Edinburgh, and indeed, she still looked quite young. According to Daniel's sire, she was the best thing that had ever happened to Uncle Logan.

They all exchanged greetings, and Logan announced, "Maggie and Will are right behind us. He moved over to the table to grab an ale, but Diana called out, "There's wine for you, if you'd prefer."

Gwyneth said, "Ooooh. Wine, Logan. Please?"

Daniel was impatient to hear the news, but Constance squeezed his hand and gave him a look he could easily interpret. *Be patient, you lout.*

Finally, once they were all settled with their drinks, he asked, "So is there any news?"

"I'll let Maggie tell you what she's uncovered," Logan replied. The amused smile on his lips indicated he had also picked up on Daniel's impatience.

Maggie and Will arrived moments later. It would have been a much more subdued entrance if not for Will's falcons. One of them tried to swoop inside after him, though they were able to usher him back out.

They all laughed over the incident as Micheil prepared them drinks. Finally, the time Daniel had been waiting for arrived.

"We have news," Maggie said.

David said, "Go ahead. We've all been waiting. Especially this one." He nodded to Daniel, who rolled his eyes.

Maggie said, "Jean MacDole somehow convinced the sheriff that she was a weak old lady who wouldn't survive being locked up, so they put her in a cellar where she was free to come and go as she pleased, although she was not allowed outside. She found some questionable characters and convinced them to go after you, Constance, with promises of bestowing great riches upon them. In her eyes, her downfall was entirely your fault because you taught Rose to stand up for herself." Maggie paused for a moment as everyone broke into applause for Constance.

"I cannot think of anything better to teach your friend, Constance," Diana said, nodding in approval. "Well done."

"She wished to repay you for all the trouble you've caused her. She was going to collect on your sale through the Channel of Dubh, and she would have received double because of your hair color. Apparently redheaded lasses are in demand."

"And now?" Uncle Logan asked. "Did they hang the bitch and put her head on a pike?"

David choked on the ale that he'd just taken a sip of.

Maggie chuckled. "Nay, but they did move her to London, where there is a separate area in the prison for females. She was not happy about the decision."

Will continued, "MacDole Castle has been officially given to Rose. We will travel to Grant land next to see what she wishes to do with it. Daniel, are you interested in traveling with us?"

Daniel let out a deep breath. "Nay. We wish to see Roddy and Rose, but there's something I must do in Edinburgh first. A young lad I made a promise to. Once I'm fit to travel, Constance and I will leave for the city."

"Are you going back to fighting, nephew?" Uncle Logan looked at him with a raised eyebrow. "I've heard about someone named Damien who was quite a fighter. There was some chatter about a devil's hand. Know anything about that?"

Daniel smirked. "Nay, I've had enough fighting. Besides, if I did that, I'd have to use Jennet's creation and someone is not fond of it." He cast a sideways glance at Constance.

Uncle Logan said, "But Jennet and Brigid worked verra hard on that."

"I'm keeping it. It's quite handy for some things, but Constance doesn't particularly care for it."

His brother laughed and added, "If you go back to fighting, it would put an end to your nickname of 'Ghost.' Everyone in Edinburgh already knows your face."

Daniel thought for a moment before he said, "I'm not sure which I prefer—Ghost or Devil's Hand."

"Ghost," Constance remarked, a bit too vehemently.

Daniel kissed her temple and said, "If it makes you happy, but I'm still keeping *Treun*. It helps me picking apples."

"You don't like it, truly? But why not, Constance?" Maggie asked.

Constance stood up to defend herself, her eyes flashing in the way he loved. "Just a moment. Please tell the entire story, husband. Make sure you tell them how your hair was unruly and matted, how your beard went untrimmed until it was disgusting, how your clothes were filthy, and you went by that name I hate. *Damien*." Her hands went to her hips.

Uncle Logan grinned at her. "Do tell us more about that. How did you know she didn't like it, Daniel?"

"Because I woke up with a dagger at my throat."

"You did not." She leaned toward him. "I was attempting to cut your beard while you slept. That way you wouldn't stop me."

Daniel quirked his brow at her as her skin turned the deepest shade of red he'd ever seen. "Your cheeks are nearly the color of your hair, wife. Is something wrong?" She must have realized what she'd said—how her words had revealed they'd slept side by side before the wedding.

Constance spun on her heel and moved over to plunk down into her chair. "Daniel, Daniel, Daniel."

Daniel reached for her hand and tugged her onto his lap.

"See, Gwynie?" Uncle Logan said happily. "She's just like you."

"Why didn't you use the name Ghost when you were fighting?" David asked.

"I didn't want the fighter to be connected to me here. Besides, I was hardly a ghost there. My aim was to be seen."

"Tell us more about the underground," David said.

"Aye, I'd like to hear more," Will agreed.

Daniel shrugged his shoulders. "There's an entire network of gambling halls where they place money on fights. Anything goes. This is their daily business, but once a moon they're called on to do more. When they receive their instructions, they send a crew out for the lasses and deliver them to a place in the east."

"Did they give you any clues as to where in the east, Daniel?" Uncle Logan asked.

"Just that it was a wealthy channel, and that it wasn't connected with any kirk or abbey. And someone made a comment that the underground was much different there. Almost as if they had lasses fighting rather than men."

His sire scoffed. "That sounds ridiculous."

Gwyneth mumbled, "Is it, Micheil? Why can they not force lasses to fight? The Norse train their women to fight."

"'Tis verra helpful, Daniel," Maggie said. "Now I have a better idea of where to send Gavin, Gregor, and Connor."

Daniel said, "Once I'm fully healed, I'll help again."

Constance said, "I will, also. Wee lassies should not have to live in fear of such a thing."

Daniel said, "We have to put an end to this, and we won't stop until we do." He leaned over and kissed his wife. "I almost lost you. When I saw you on Lamont's horse, I thought I would vomit for sure."

"I'm never leaving you, Daniel. I promise."

"Good," he said as he reached over and caressed the back of her neck. "Because if you do, I'll turn into Damien again. It was a wild ride for a few days." He waggled his eyebrows at her.

Constance glared at him.

CHAPTER TWENTY-NINE

D ANIEL AND CONSTANCE HEADED DOWN the middle of Edinburgh on horseback. Daniel hoped no one would recognize him, especially since he'd gone out of his way to groom himself, trimming his beard and his hair. This time he proudly wore his Drummond plaid. He couldn't help but smirk at his wife.

"Why are you laughing, Daniel? I know that look," Constance whispered.

"'Tis naught."

"Out with it. I know I had something to do with that thought." She gave him her elbow, easy enough to do since she was seated in front of him.

"I was just thinking how I'd never dare *not* to trim my hair or beard for fear I'd awaken to a dagger at my throat again."

She chuckled. "Aye, 'tis true, though you know I was only holding the dagger there to trim your beard."

"So you keep insisting." He stopped his horse near the village stables, dismounted, then helped his wife down.

"Daniel, I hope we find him," she said softly. "The lad looked like he could use friends. Where do we start?"

"We'll find him." He spoke to the man in the stable about taking care of his horse, tossed him a coin. "You know a lad named Terric?" he asked. "Used to sleep here."

"Aye, still does on occasion. He comes back to help us."

"Do you know where I can find him?"

The man tipped his head toward the castle. "Usually near the castle. He's always looking to pick up more coin."

Daniel took Constance by the hand and headed toward the castle, not far away. When they arrived, he stood in the cobblestone courtyard and glanced around. A voice called out to him, "My lord, my lord! Wait, my lord!"

Daniel pivoted just in time to see the lad launch himself into his arms. "Terric! You are hale, lad?"

"Aye, you dinnae forget me. I feared you would." Terric's bright eyes glittered in the noonday sun. "Greetings, my lady."

"You are well, lad?"

"Aye, and I have something of yours, my lord." Terric asked, "Come with me?"

"Lead the way." Daniel wrapped his arm around Constance's waist.

When they were nearly back by the stables, Terric said, "Wait here." Then he disappeared down the street.

Daniel took a moment to look around at the city, his mind returning to the time when he'd fought for coin and loved it. A small twinge of regret caught him, but he knew he'd made the right decision. For the short time he'd been involved in the underground fighting circuit, he'd felt stronger, more like a normal, whole man. He recognized it now for false confidence, but he'd learned from the experience.

A man strode by him, but then stopped in his tracks, turning around to stare at him. "Are you not the Devil's Hand?" His finger moved to his chin and he scratched, leveling his gaze at Daniel. "Aye? You look almost exactly like him."

"He's my brother," Daniel lied, not wishing to bring any undue attention to Constance.

"That explains it. If you see him, tell him to come back. No one fights like he did. I'd still wager on him."

"I'll tell him," Daniel said, shooting a grin at Constance.

She stared back at him with wide eyes.

Terric came down the path a moment later, a package in his hand, beaming. "Here. I saved it for you."

Daniel tore the twine off and dropped the wrapping, surprised to see his bags of coin. "Terric, you saved these all this time? Why did you not use it to pay for the inn or for your food? 'Twould have been acceptable." He took the bag of coins and held it up for Constance to see.

"What is it, Daniel?" Constance asked.

"'Tis all the coin I won fighting. I mostly forgot about it, but I gave it to Terric to watch. I thought you'd use it to live on, lad." He pulled out a few coins and gave them to him. "At least you'll take this for saving the bags for me. Go get yourself a meat pie and come back." Terric didn't need to be asked twice—he took off toward a street vendor not far away.

"Daniel, 'tis quite a bit of coin," Constance said. "You'd better hide it."

He gave Constance a bag and said, "I know you cannot replace the stone you lost, but mayhap you can purchase something else that will remind you of your mother. Surely you would not have lost it if not for me."

She stared at the coin, her eyes misting.

"What is it?" he asked, peering at her because it was such an odd thing to cry over.

"Daniel, I'll sound daft, but when I look at Terric, and I think about wee Kelby at the abbey, it makes me wish we could do something to help all the bairns who are different. Terric is missing a hand, Kelby doesn't walk right. She'll always limp and no one will want her. Could we not do something for the wee ones who are misfits? Could we use this coin to help them in some way?"

Daniel stared at his wee wife, thinking about how much he adored her. She had the biggest heart of anyone he'd ever met. "I just had a thought. I'm going to send a message to Roddy. See if he'll meet us near Braden's."

"Oh, good. I'd so love to see dear Rose again. What are you thinking?"

Terric came running back with a lad a few years younger than he was. The lad was also missing a hand. "This is my friend. Do you mind if he eats with me?"

"Not at all," Constance said. "Terric, is your friend without parents, too?"

"Aye. I saw the other lads teasing him one day…"

"Terric saved me," the lad said, smiling. "My name's Henry. My mother was English, but she died."

"How did you lose your hand, Henry?"

"I got caught stealing food for my mother before she passed away. My father could not feed us so I stole a bag of oats. The sheriff caught me and chopped off my hand. Then my father sent me out. He did not want a cripple."

Daniel nearly choked with a raw fury, but he quickly hid it. None of it was the lad's fault. "How would you lads like to go for a journey with us? We're heading into the Highlands. We still have time before the heavy snows fly."

Terric looked to his friend, who was emphatically nodding his head. "May we both come?"

"Aye. Once you finish your meal, gather your belongings and meet me at the stable. I'm going to stop and send a message first, then I'll get you a horse. I promise we'll feed you well."

Constance gave him a questioning look, but he just kissed her cheek and said, "Trust me, lass. 'Twill be my wedding gift to you. I know 'tis a bit late, but I wished to wait until 'twas perfect."

Henry and Terric stared at each other, their eyes glittering with excitement, before they took off to grab their belongings.

"I'm telling everyone you picked me to help with your journey," Henry announced over his shoulder.

"Oh, Daniel," Constance murmured, "When we find our own home, can we not make it big enough to welcome in some of these bairns? I could ask Ada to help. We could think of something." She'd told him about Ada— how she'd become much kinder after Rose saved her and the other lasses from being sold.

"I've already got a plan. Your heart is so big you've given me the idea." Daniel patted her hand and said, "Patience, lass. Patience. Though I know 'tis not your strongest quality."

"Nor is it yours," she said, raising an eyebrow.

"Aye, you do know me."

———◆———

WHEN THE FOUR FINALLY ARRIVED at Muir Castle just after nightfall, they couldn't wait to get inside away from the bitter wind. They'd taken their time, so the voyage had stretched out for a few days, but now Constance felt as if she was frozen inside and out.

"I hope Braden has the fire going," she whispered to Daniel. "Poor Henry is shivering as I am."

Daniel helped her dismount, kissing her lips quickly. "Aye, you are an ice queen at the moment if your lips are any indication, but I do promise to warm you tonight."

"Will we have a chamber or pallets in the great hall? Or mayhap even a cottage?" Constance whimpered through her shivers.

"They'll have a chamber for us. You've been to the keep before. 'Tis quite big and beautiful."

"Aye, 'tis true. Lads, Steenie is younger than you two, but he'll be pleased to have visitors. You can probably sleep with him this eve. He has a pony, too, and I'm sure he'd love to show Paddy to you on the morrow."

Henry grew wide-eyed and asked, "Not in the stables? Not on the ground somewhere?" Then he glanced at Terric. "I've never slept inside before."

"Not even at home, Henry?" Constance asked, afraid to hear his answer.

"Nay, the lads slept in the stables with the horse and the pigs."

Braden and Roddy came out to greet them. "So glad to see you both," Braden said, "and you've brought friends."

"Aye, Terric is the taller and Henry is the shorter. Come, lads. Inside and up close to the hearth."

Once they stepped inside, Rose squealed and raced over to greet her. Constance grabbed her friend, wrapping her arms around her. "Oh, Rose, I'm so happy to see you. Are you happy?"

When they finally found the will to separate, Rose said, "I'm verra happy. I hear you and Daniel have married! I was so hoping you would." Then she whispered in her friend's ear, "He's perfect for you."

Constance nodded in agreement. "I know."

Rose squeezed her hand and announced, "I have news for you."

Constance moved over to greet Cairstine, who quickly said, "You are all so cold. Come by the fire. Steenie, take the lads into the kitchens and find something for all of us to eat. Grandmama just went inside." The lads had started chattering as soon as they met one another, so they followed their orders happily enough.

The adults settled in around the hearth, conversing about the weather and all that had transpired. Constance noticed that Roddy had pulled Daniel aside and they'd whispered together before returning to the group with big smiles on their faces.

Constance couldn't stand the suspense. "Out with it! What is it you two have planned?"

Roddy said, "Rose and I have been discussing our plans for the future, and Daniel just gave us the answers to our prayers."

Rose bolted out of her seat. "He did?"

"Please tell us all," Constance said.

Rose pivoted to the group and clapped her hands

together. "Roddy and I have been given MacDole Castle. At first, I did not think I could live there, but now that some time has passed, I miss my home. We were hoping we could convince Daniel and Constance to come live with us. We'd be so close to Braden and Cairstine. Roddy, Daniel, and Braden could continue to work with the Band of Cousins—" she grinned at Constance, "—and I'd have my dear friend with me."

Daniel took a step forward and said, "I just suggested my idea to Roddy, and he loves it."

"What is it, Daniel?" Constance held her breath because she was so excited.

"Constance, with her big heart, gave me the idea when we were in Edinburgh. Both of us wish to do more for Terric and Henry, and I know Constance would like to be reunited with wee Kelby at the abbey. The lassie has a limp and will probably never walk right. Our cousin Loki has a home for orphans. He welcomes them inside, and they all contribute and live together. I was wondering about doing the same for bairns who were lacking, misfits for lack of a better word. Roddy and Rose have the place but not the coin. Constance and I have the coin but not the place. What if we make MacDole Castle the Castle for Misfits? Terric, Henry, and Kelby can all move in with us. Be part of our clan, a special clan."

"Oh, Daniel. 'Tis a wonderful idea. What do you think, Rose?" How she hoped her dear friend would agree.

Her friend's radiant smile was answer enough. "I love the idea! We can journey there on the morrow and see how the place has fared in our absence. The furnishings are still there. We would just have to clean, buy some supplies, though we had many foodstuffs stored in the cellars already. There were turnips and apples and barley already there."

Constance moved over and gave Daniel a hug. "What a lovely idea, Daniel. But I don't want to call them misfits.

Mayhap they were misfits, but they will be misfits no longer. We'll come up with another name for the castle."

They all thought for a moment, then Constance said,
"'Twill be a special home for special bairns. How about
the Home for Special Bairns?"

The others cheered her suggestion, and Constance
sighed in satisfaction. All of her dreams had come true.

EPILOGUE

———◆———

A sennight later in West Lothian

GAVIN AND GREGOR RODE THEIR horses out on their usual patrol around Ramsay land, searching for any reivers or prowlers.

Nothing. Another boring patrol.

Gavin sighed deeply. "I'm ready to go."

"Where to?" asked his best friend and cousin.

"Anywhere. Are you not tired of staying at home after all the excitement we've been involved in of late? The fight with those bastards on Loch Linnhe, the black pool…gambling in Edinburgh and watching Daniel pummel every fighter in the land? The falcons, the owl, even Paddy the Pony. There's more out there in life than what we'll find on Ramsay land, Gregor. Can you not feel it? We need to leave, and soon. We're *supposed* to leave."

Gregor, the more serious of the two, quirked his brow at his friend. "You are not fooling me. You're jealous you don't have a lassie of your own. I know how you are with lasses."

Gavin snorted, staring up at the swirling gray clouds overhead, the wind picking up in intensity. "Mayhap, but none of the lasses in our clan interest me."

"Then who would?"

"Hmmm. A lass who's lean and strong, a fighter."

Gregor laughed. "You've just described your mother."

Gavin tugged on the reins of his horse, charging toward his cousin. "I'll kick your arse if I ever hear you say that again. I do not want someone like my mother. Damn you for suggesting it."

Gregor set his horse to galloping and shouted over his shoulder, "Your words, not mine." His laughter could be heard over the horses' hooves.

As they raced along—a usual pastime for them—Gavin cursed under his breath. He had to admit Gregor was right about something, although he certainly did *not* wish to find a lass like his mother. Hellfire, nay, his mother gave him enough trouble. But he *was* interested in finding a lass of his own. He slowed his horse and Gregor, who'd easily kept pace, did the same. Once they caught their breath, he asked, "Do you not find it odd that all our cousins have married of late? Braden, Roddy, Daniel. They all married within a few moons of one another, and none of them had a large clan wedding."

"'Tis unusual, aye, but it does not make me feel I must marry. Why does it bother you so?"

"Because we've lost most of our band. Who will go with us to seek out the kidnappers now? I wish to find all those bastards."

"You raise a good point. I'm sure Maggie and Will have thought of some way for us to be of assistance. We just have to wait for their return from Edinburgh. Mayhap they've learned more from our king." Gregor turned his horse around and headed back toward the keep, their patrol finished.

Gavin spurred ahead of his cousin. "I'm not interested in waiting."

———◆———

LOGAN RAMSAY ALWAYS MADE A boisterous entrance, so when the door of the keep banged open loudly enough for the sound to echo off the rafters, Gavin knew his sire had arrived before he even looked.

He bolted off the bench where he and Gregor had been munching their late meal. "Papa. Gregor and I wish to speak with you."

His sire nodded to Gregor before shifting his gaze back to Gavin, "What is it?"

"We wish to head northeast to ferret out the other kidnappers in the Channel of Dubh. We plan to leave on the morrow."

His sire snorted, which was not a promising sign. "Nay, you're not, and stop blaming Gregor for your ideas. I know you're the one who wishes to go. I'll say it again in case you did not hear me the first time. Nay."

"Why not?"

"You don't know the northeast, and none of your cousins are available to travel with you. What more do you need to know?"

"I'll take guards with me."

"Nay. End of story. You'll wait until your sister comes home." His sire spun on his heel and headed toward the kitchens, a loud bang punctuating his departure.

Gregor shrugged his shoulders. "I'm not surprised he didn't go along with it. You don't know where you're going. Your sire hates it when we jump into plans without being prepared."

Gavin's gaze narrowed as he stared after the departing figure of his sire. "I could learn. My sister isn't the only one capable of rooting out information."

"Mayhap not, but you can't deny she's good at it. Promise me you'll wait until Maggie and Will return. They're supposed to arrive any day."

Gavin thought for a moment then said, "I'll give them a few days. If they're not back by then, I'm leaving, whether you wish to go with me or not." He stared at his hands for a few moments and said, "Something bad is happening in the northeast. That part of the Channel of Dubh is the worst."

Gregor dropped the bone he was chewing on. "How the hell do you know that?"

"I don't know, but I do. 'Tis worse than any of the others." He sighed. "You'll see."

He hadn't intended it to sound like a promise.

~ THE END ~

DEAR READERS,

Thank you for reading Daniel's story. I enjoyed their tale because they are such a fun couple.

As many historical romance and fiction authors do, when I began my research, I found the Legend of the Lee Penny. It is a tale about a red amulet, triangular in shape (heart-shaped) that was brought back from the Crusades in 1330 by Sir Symon Locard. It is mounted on a coin, and if you search the internet, you'll find the story of the Lee Penny and its medicinal qualities.

There is no mention of the coin before 1330, when it was given to Sir Symon Locard, who dubbed it the Lee Penny. So I created my own version of where it could have originated and how it became lost.

My version is completely fictional, just another creation of my mind. I like to think that if it were lost this way, it would eventually find its way back to its original owners.

Next up in the Band of Cousins is Gavin's story.

Happy reading!

As always, reviews would be greatly appreciated. Sign up for my newsletter on my website at *www.keiramontclair.com*. I send newsletters out with each new release.

Another way to receive notices about my new releases is to follow me on BookBub. Click on the tab in the upper right-hand side of my profile page. You can also write a review on this platform.

Keira Montclair

www.keiramontclair.com
www.facebook.com/KeiraMontclair
www.pinterest.com/KeiraMontclair

Novels by

Keira Montclair

———◆———

THE BAND OF COUSINS
HIGHLAND VENGEANCE
HIGHLAND ABDUCTION
HIGHLAND RETRIBUTION
HIGHLAND LIES
HIGHLAND FORTITUDE

THE CLAN GRANT SERIES
#1- RESCUED BY A HIGHLANDER-
Alex and Maddie
#2- HEALING A HIGHLANDER'S HEART-
Brenna and Quade
#3- LOVE LETTERS FROM LARGS-
Brodie and Celestina
#4-JOURNEY TO THE HIGHLANDS-
Robbie and Caralyn
#5-HIGHLAND SPARKS-
Logan and Gwyneth
#6-MY DESPERATE HIGHLANDER-
Micheil and Diana
#7-THE BRIGHTEST STAR IN
THE HIGHLANDS-
Jennie and Aedan

#8- HIGHLAND HARMONY-
Avelina and Drew

THE HIGHLAND CLAN
LOKI-Book One
TORRIAN-Book Two
LILY-Book Three
JAKE-Book Four
ASHLYN-Book Five
MOLLY-Book Six
JAMIE AND GRACIE- Book Seven
SORCHA-Book Eight
KYLA-Book Nine
BETHIA-Book Ten
LOKI'S CHRISTMAS STORY-Book Eleven

THE SOULMATE CHRONICLES
#1-TRUSTING A HIGHLANDER

THE SUMMERHILL SERIES-
CONTEMPORARY ROMANCE
#1-ONE SUMMERHILL DAY
#2-A FRESH START FOR TWO
#3-THREE REASONS TO LOVE

STAND-ALONE NOVEL
FALLING FOR THE CHIEFTAIN-Book Three in
Enchanted Falls Trilogy

ABOUT THE AUTHOR

KEIRA MONTCLAIR is the pen name of an author who lives in Florida with her husband. She loves to write fast-paced, emotional romance, especially with children as secondary characters in her stories.

She has worked as a registered nurse in pediatrics and recovery room nursing. Teaching is another of her loves, and she has taught both high school mathematics and practical nursing.

Now she loves to spend her time writing, but there isn't enough time to write everything she wants! Her Highlander Clan Grant series, comprising of eight standalone novels, is a reader favorite. Her third series, The Highland Clan, set twenty years after the Clan Grant series, focuses on the Grant/Ramsay descendants. She also has a contemporary series set in The Finger Lakes of Western New York and a paranormal historical series, The Soulmate Chronicles.

Contact her through her website, *www.keiramontclair.com*

www.ingramcontent.com/pod-product-compliance
Lightning Source LLC
Chambersburg PA
CBHW061133200626

46817CB00016B/1317